The Girl Who Found Christmas

An Advent Calendar Storybook

by

Barbara Escher

Acknowledgments

First, last, and always, I am so grateful to my husband, Joe Merkt, for his support and encouragement as I struggled to bring Belinda to life. He believed in me–and in the story–and I am so grateful.

And I am deeply grateful to my first readers. My daughter, Rachel Fisher, who is a talented novelist. My friend and writing mentor Terri Lewis. They encouraged me to let Belinda be Belinda, let her make a mistake sometimes. And let her be silly. And above all, make sure she never forgets to ask questions three at a time!

Dayne Sislen, who created the beautiful cover and the chapter illustrations of the book, deserves special thanks. I wasn't sure anyone would see the Belinda that I saw. But Dayne saw and captured a child who almost exploded with life, energy, and joy.

David Aretha, Editor Extraordinaire, helped me align the words with the story. After years of business writing, it was hard for me to tell a story for young children without using big words! David helped me match the words to the story, and I am so thankful. Otherwise, I would have to hope that seventh graders would fall in love with Belinda!

Last but not least, I would like to express my hopes that the children of military families would feel less alone if they could talk to "Howard" about the loved ones who are far away, on Christmas and throughout the year.

An Advent Calendar Storybook

by
Barbara Escher

Red Mitten Books

PRINTED IN THE U.S.A.

Introduction

If your kids love opening an Advent Calendar every night in December, imagine how much they will love a Christmas bedtime story every night—especially a mystery story!

Every day in December, a little girl named Belinda has an important secret job: her mom has asked her to be a Christmas Detective. And Belinda's job is to figure out what Christmas is all about and keep track of what she has learned every single day. You know—FIND CHRISTMAS—before Christmas Eve!

Six-year-old Belinda has almost everything a little girl could want—a comfortable home with her dad and Gramps and a fluffy cat named Custard. She likes living in the country outside of Philadelphia.

Belinda's dad and Gramps take good care of her, but her mom takes care of sick soldiers far away and may not get home in time for Christmas, so Belinda really, really wants to solve her mom's mystery and FIND CHRISTMAS before Christmas Eve!

Like a good detective, she keeps track of what she has figured out every single day and draws a picture to show her mom. But being a detective is a big job! Some days, Belinda thinks Christmas is a reindeer, or a tree, or Santa, or making a snowman.

One snowy night, while Belinda is busy detecting and drawing pictures, Custard sneaks out and gets lost in the snow. Belinda is desperate to find him before he freezes, and Custard's story becomes an important chapter in Belinda's search for Christmas.

Belinda asks for help in solving the mystery every morning from someone whom she calls "Howard." Don't tell Belinda, but most people don't call Him "Howard"—they call Him God. Belinda started calling Him Howard when she was very little and tried to say the Lord's Prayer. Somehow, "Hallowed be Thy Name" was just too hard to say. But "Howard be Thy name" was just right. And "Howard" it remains even to this very day.

We hope your child will draw along with Belinda and join her on a nightly journey to Find Christmas!

Barbara Escher

Dedicated to the parents, grandparents, teachers, librarians and unofficial family members who nurture joy, courage, enthusiasm, and curiosity in the children whose lives they touch.

The Girl Who Found Christmas:
An Advent Calendar Storybook

Published by Red Mitten Books, U.S.A.

For information address Red Mitten Books, Publisher, 4222 W. Bay View Avenue, Tampa, Florida 33611
www.redmittenbooks.com

First edition

Hardcover edition: 978-1-7333034-1-5
Paperback edition: 978-1-7333034-3-9
EPub edition: 978-1-7333034-0-8

Library of Congress Control Number 2019911916
Cataloging-in-publication Data
Escher, Barbara. "The Girl Who Found Christmas"

Cover and interior design by Dayne Sislen.
The artwork in this book was created in multiple media:
pencil, crayons and Adobe Photoshop.

Table of Contents

December 1: Meet Belinda

Welcome to 1234 Old River Road! The girl who lives here is six years old, and she loves the bright red front door on her house. It reminds her of her own bright, curly red hair! The little girl's name is Belinda, and she always has a very big smile when she comes home and sees that red door.

Another thing about her house that makes Belinda smile is the rumbly sound of the pipes. She knows what that noise means! Sometimes those old rumbly pipes have to work extra hard to keep the farmhouse warm for her family and for Custard, her kitty, during cold winter nights. Shhh! Let's meet Belinda!

"Howard," whispered Belinda, "I think my toes is froze."

Wiggling her toes, Belinda grinned at her cat, Custard, as he jumped off the bed. "What's the matter, Custard, you silly cat?" But Custard did not answer. He simply waved his fluffy tail proudly as he made his way to his own warm bed.

"Uh-oh," Belinda giggled. "Looks like talking to You and wiggling my toes woke up Custard, and he's pretty mad. I'm sorry he doesn't say 'Good morning' to You, but it's okay. I can say 'Good morning' for both of us."

Snuggling down in her warm bed with all her toes under the covers, she whispered, "Good morning, Howard! Thank you for my warm bed and for that crazy kitty and for something that smells good in the kitchen. I can tell it's going to be a GREAT day, and I hope You have a good day too. Love You!"

Belinda was very accustomed to talking to God and calling Him Howard (like Howard be Thy Name). She wanted to make God feel a little closer (especially while her mother was away). Calling Him Howard made it seem like He was just right there. And she didn't think He'd mind.

With her quick morning prayer out of the way, she jumped out of bed in one swift movement, grabbing her fluffy yellow robe on the way to the door. But she didn't get very far!

"COLD, COLD, COLD!" she said as she turned back to her room to get her slippers. While she was there, she slowed down just long enough to give her favorite pictures a pat. "Great picture, dude," she whispered to the picture of Custard the Dragon. Custard the Dragon's story was special to Belinda because the little girl in that story was named—what else?—Belinda!

Next to the picture of Custard the Dragon hung a picture of Belinda with her mom and dad. "Hi, Mommy," she whispered. "I love that you have curly red hair and big green eyes and freckles like me. And Daddy has glasses and straight sticky-up brown hair and brown eyes like Gramps. We're all different, but we're a family just the same. Except, maybe, for Custard," she giggled. "He isn't tall like Daddy or short like Mommy. He's not even as short as me!"

She stopped again on her way to the door. Something was different about the calendar on the wall. It still showed a big picture of a snowy house in the country. But the calendar said it was December 1!

"Dad! Gramps!" she shouted as she raced toward the kitchen. "It's December. That means Christmas. And that means presents. And Santa. And Baby Jesus. Oh boy oh boy oh boy!"

"Whoa!!" Belinda's dad said as the little girl flew into his arms. "Good morning, Belinda! You are full speed ahead this morning!"

"Yes," said Belinda, her bright green eyes shining. "AND," she said, "I have THREE reasons!"

"Of course you do," said Gramps, looking nice and warm in his flannel shirt as he carefully turned the hot bacon in the skillet. "You ALWAYS have three reasons!"

Walking to the stove and wiggling her nose with delight, Belinda said, "First, I smell BACON. Second, today is DECEMBER. And third, December means Christmas and presents and Baby Jesus."

"Wow," her father said. "All good reasons to be full speed ahead. And I have another one for you! The last time I talked to your mom on

Skype, she asked me to wait until today—the first day of December—and then ask YOU a question."

"Oh fooey!" said Belinda, pulling out a chair. "I didn't get to talk to her again! I wish Skype would keep track of what time I'm at school. I have so many questions for HER too!"

Before she could slide her feet under the table, Belinda's dad said, "How about if you wash your hands and come to the table for pancakes and bacon? Looks like Gramps made a feast for us!"

Running down the hall to the bathroom, Belinda called over her shoulder, "I'm washing and hurrying! Don't start telling the question without me!"

Gramps chuckled and shook his head, putting the crispy bacon on plates and carrying a stack of golden pancakes to the table.

With everyone in their chairs, Gramps asked God to bless their food. While waiting for the "Amen," Belinda wrinkled her nose like a bunny and sniffed the smell of bacon, which was a rare treat in her house.

"Amen," said Gramps. "Oh boy!" said Belinda, staring hard at her father. "Bacon and pancakes and questions! I think I like questions even more than I like—well—maybe not QUITE as much as I like bacon, but I like questions a whole lot!"

With just the tiniest bit of bacon in her mouth, Belinda mumbled, "So Mom is okay? And does she miss me? And is it December where she is too?"

Washing down the bacon with a glass of milk to avoid the usual

"Don't talk with food in your mouth," she waited impatiently for answers.

"Okay, Belinda. First, your mom is okay. Of course she misses you. And it is definitely December where she is."

Tucking another piece of bacon in her mouth, Belinda sighed and swallowed. "That's a relief," said Belinda before she remembered what her father had said. "You said she wanted you to ask ME a question? Are you sure it wasn't THREE questions?" she giggled.

"No," Belinda's father said. "Just one. But it's an important one. And your mother and I think that answering the question should be part of every single day from now until Christmas."

"Like making cookies?" Belinda hoped.

"Not exactly," her father said.

"So what is the question that I have to answer every single day?" Belinda asked. "Is it hard, like a school question? Do I need to write it down?"

"Well," her father replied, "it isn't easy. And you don't have to write it down. But it's very important."

"Okay, okay, okay," said Belinda, folding her hands and wrinkling her face like a very serious student. "I am ready for the question!"

Belinda's father smiled at her, then sat down and took his daughter's hands. "The question is: What is it that makes it Christmas?"

"You mean I have to FIND Christmas?" Belinda asked, scrunching her forehead.

"Well, it's not missing," her father said. "But that's the idea. You have to figure out what it's really all about."

"Oh boy," said Belinda, shaking her mop of curls. "I don't suppose Mom sent me any clues or treasure maps?"

"No," her father laughed. "But she suggested that you might draw something every day when you think of a clue, so you can share it with her."

"Like a make-your-own treasure map," Belinda mumbled. Then, grinning, she said, "But I can do it. Maybe I will start right away!!"

December 2: A Hard Question

Welcome to another day at 1234 Old River Road! What do we know about Belinda so far? Hmm. She has green eyes AND freckles and red hair (like her red front door). She likes to ask questions in THREES. She loves bacon when her Gramps makes it. (Actually, she loves bacon any time.) I wonder if she got started on answering her mom's question? Let's find out!

"Good morning, Howard," whispered Belinda as she woke to another cold morning. "I tried very hard yesterday to think about my mom's question, but I don't think I have the answer yet. Maybe today You could help me come up with more ideas!"

Warming up her toes, she continued, "My mom sent me paper and crayons to make an Advent Calendar with ideas of what makes it Christmas. I think Dad's working at home on his computer today, so maybe I can sit in his office and draw some answers. I really LOVE Christmas and want it to be perfect, perfect, perfect this year. But I don't know exactly what it is that MAKES it Christmas!"

Rolling over, she pictured the Advent Calendar she would make, filling it with things she loved to do at Christmastime—like decorating the tree, making cookies, and other stuff.

"Howard," she said firmly, I am going to start my calendar with a picture of a Christmas tree. But if You could help me with some more ideas before tonight, that would be very good!

"And I hope YOU have a super day today. Love YOU!"

With that, Belinda tumbled her kitty onto the floor and jumped out of bed as fast as she could, ready to begin the second day of December.

Scooting to the breakfast table in a hurry, as usual, Belinda said, "Daddy, I asked Howard about Mom's question and asked Him to help me figure out the answer. I don't think that's cheating, like asking someone about a question on a test at school. What do you think?"

Belinda's dad adjusted his glasses and said, "Of course it's okay to ask Howard for help. In fact, it's an excellent idea and definitely not cheating."

Pouring coffee for himself and Gramps, he continued, "I wonder, Belinda, if you know that I often ask Howard for help myself and so does your mom."

"Me too," said Gramps, carrying the mugs to the table.

"Gramps," said Belinda, "did you ever ask Howard for help when you were a vet and you had sick animals to take care of?"

"Absolutely," Gramps said, sipping his coffee and hanging up his baseball cap. "Sometimes a dog or a cat or even a horse was really sick or injured, and I asked for all the help I could get. I didn't get horses in our barn very often, but sometimes they needed help in a hurry and couldn't wait to get to the Large Animal Vet."

Chewing her toast, Belinda said, "Well, I hope my mom is asking Howard if she can come home soon. My best friend Elizabeth AND my friend Andrew asked me how come my mom is never home. I told them that she is a doctor and she's away taking care of soldiers who are very hurt, but that she'll be home as soon as she can."

Remembering that she was going to be in trouble for talking with her mouth full, Belinda swallowed her toast and continued, "BUT, DAD, Elizabeth said that there are lots of sick people here, so why can't Mommy be home with us and take care of sick people too?"

Taking a sip of coffee, Belinda's dad glanced across the table at Gramps and said to Belinda, "I think it's time for you to talk to your mom about where she is and what she's doing. How about if we Skype her when you get home from school? At three o'clock our time, it will be about nine o'clock where she is. I'm going to be working from home most of the day, so I'll send her a message to let her know that she should expect our call."

"HURRAY!!" Belinda said. "I love it when we Skype! And I can show her my Advent Calendar too!"

School seemed to take forever that day as Belinda thought about talking to her mom. She was bouncing in her seat and wishing for a fidget spinner before it was even lunchtime. At last it was time to go home, and she was out the door so fast, her snowflake parka looked like a blur as she ran to the bus.

At home, her father had Skype ready to go and was already chatting with Belinda's mother. They were catching up on the boring things that grown-ups talk about.

Belinda flew in the door, dropping her parka as she ran to the desk. There she saw her mother's face on the screen, just as her dad had promised.

"Mommy!" she shouted. "It's really you and I can really see you!"

Laughing, her mother said, "And I can really see you too, Belinda. How was your day at school today?"

"Not great," Belinda said, looking at the screen. "This yucky boy named Denny doinged my hair—you know, Mom. He pulled on a curl and let it go and said DOING like he was so cool!"

"And what did you do about it, Belinda?" her mother asked.

"I told him I would DOING his nose if he ever did it again, and the teacher came over and told him that it wasn't okay. But, you know, curly hair isn't always easy!"

"I know!" said her mother. "Boys would DOING my curls too when I was your age. And sometimes they asked if all my freckles would ever stick together! It's not always easy to have curly hair and freckles, is it, Belinda?"

"No, Mommy, it's not easy! But I like having curly red hair and freckles just like you!"

Interrupting, Belinda's father, Sam, said, "We don't have a lot of time, Belinda. Your mother still has some things to do tonight, and you have work to do on your Advent Calendar. So let's make sure that you get an answer to your question right away."

"Belinda," her mom said, "Elizabeth is right that there are sick people in our town too. But the only way I could become a doctor was to promise that I would take care of sick soldiers for a while. It's not forever. But it's important that I keep my promise."

"Oh!" Belinda said.

"People make small promises all the time, Belinda. You help clean up the kitchen when you want extra bacon! That's a great promise! You are getting something you want a whole lot—like bacon. Or a sleepover."

"I made a BIG promise—bigger than bacon!!" she chuckled. "I get to be a doctor forever, but for a little while longer, I have to keep my promise and take care of our soldiers. Does that make sense to you, Belinda?"

Belinda turned and looked at her mother. Her father saw the look and realized his daughter's eyes had gotten wide and still. When she finally spoke, Belinda said, "So do you go places where you might get sick too?"

"No," her mother said. "I am in a safe place, but our soldiers and the people who live here will need help for a little while longer, until a new doctor can come here and take over."

Swallowing a big lump in her throat, Belinda said, "Thank you for telling me, Mommy. I miss you an awful, awful lot, but I'm lucky to have Dad and Gramps and Custard and Elizabeth and Andrew till you get back."

Her mother chuckled. "I suspect you and Custard are keeping everyone busy! I have to hurry now and get some things done. I hope it's okay if I see your Advent Calendar the next time I call? Love you till the butter flies!" she said as she winked and signed off.

Grabbing her paper and crayons, Belinda couldn't wait to draw a picture on her Advent Calendar. Maybe today it would be the Christmas tree, or a picture of her daddy or some soldiers who were sick? Heading for the kitchen table, she said, "I wonder if they have Christmas trees where Mom is? I'll bet she will like MY Christmas tree the best!

December 3:
The First Present

Belinda is SO glad that she can tell her friends why her mom is so far away. She can even tell them about the important promise. And about how her mom will come home to 1234 Old River Road to be with Belinda and her father and Gramps and Custard as soon as the new doctor is there to take care of the soldiers. Belinda can hardly wait!

"Good morning, Howard," whispered a sleepy Belinda. "I'm missing my mom today and hope You are taking very good care of her. I had a dream about her, and she gave me the biggest hug ever. But then I woke up." Her usual smile dimmed as she thought about how long it had been since she'd had a real hug from her mom.

"Howard," she continued, staring at her star-speckled bedroom ceiling, "last night I tried again to think about my mom's question. You know: What is it that makes it Christmas? And I drew a picture of my mom and some soldiers standing next to a big, fat Christmas tree! I gave her curly red hair and green eyes just like me.

"But THAT made me wonder some more. So I thought about what we always DO on Christmas Eve, and one day I will draw some Christmas stockings too, even though I don't ACTUALLY think it's stockings that make it Christmas."

Sighing, she rolled onto her belly and planted her face in the pillow. "Humph," she mumbled. "I forgot to say thank You for yesterday. Getting to talk to my mom on Skype was great. I'm sad about the sick soldiers, but I'm glad that Mommy can help them get better."

Rolling over again, she thought about what her mommy said about second chances.

"Howard," Belinda said, "my mommy said that sometimes people make mistakes or bad things happen, but they can get second chances. Especially if they fix their mistakes and try harder. Do you think Santa gives extra chances on the naughty and nice list? I always try hard to be nice, but sometimes I'm crabby or don't listen to my dad the first time. I guess Mommy says I might get a second chance to do better."

With that, she bounced out of bed, said a loud, "THANK YOU, HOWARD, AND HAVE A GREAT DAY!" and headed out the door toward breakfast.

"Good morning, Belinda!" said her father as his barefoot daughter wrapped him in an extra-powerful hug. "You are Wonder Woman strong this morning."

"Good morning, Dad," she said, leaning into his broad chest. "I dreamed that Mom gave me a giant hug, and it reminded me that I miss her a lot, so I wanted to hug you extra special this morning."

Holding his daughter close, Sam glanced at Belinda's grandfather. They all missed Belinda's mom and could hardly wait for the day when she would be home again.

"I thought about hugging Custard," Belinda mumbled, "but I don't think Custard likes hugs very much. Maybe we should get a puppy?" she asked, peeking up at her father with a twinkle in her eye.

"Probably not before breakfast," her father chuckled. "And speaking of breakfast…"

"I know, I know," said Belinda. "I smell cinnamon French toast! Am I too late? Can I help? I don't even mind getting eggy mess on my fingers!"

Laughing, her father said, "If you wash your hands quickly, you can help with the last batch."

No one ever had to ask Belinda twice to do something fun! Her dad already had a big white bowl with mushed-up egg and a little bit of milk inside. But Belinda got to dredge (a funny word, according to Belinda) slices of bread in the mush. She also got to sprinkle the cinnamon on top before plopping the bread onto the griddle.

"Nice job, Belinda," Gramps said, glancing over his shoulder with a smile as he set the table. "Looks like you got over the yucky part and are enjoying making breakfast. Good for you!"

Turning from the stove for a moment, Belinda smiled at Gramps and said, "Just wait till you taste my French toast, Gramps! You and Daddy make great pancakes, but my French toast will be super awesome good!"

"I have no doubt," her grandfather said with a smile.

"So what are we going to do tonight?" Belinda asked between bites.

"Well," her father said, "you could draw more pictures on your Advent Calendar to show your mom the next time we Skype her."

"Yessss!! And we could talk to Mommy about the puppy at the same time!"

"I know you are thinking about a puppy, so you will have something else to hug," her dad said. "And I know Custard does not like hugs. But I can think of someone else in your life you might like to hug."

Belinda looked up at her father, counting on her fingers and trying to guess. "Well, YOU of course," she said. "And Gramps, who's YOUR dad. And my friend Elizabeth. And Andrew. And Grandmother, who's Mommy's mom."

"Funny you should mention Grandmother," Belinda's father said. "She sent a package for you and said that you may open it right away." Reaching into the closet, Belinda's father pulled out a brightly colored box and said (in his teasing voice), "Of course you could save it for Christmas if you want to."

"Now, now, now!" said Belinda, reaching for the box and jumping up and down with excitement.

Gently shaking the box, she said, "It's BEAUTIFUL! And I know it can't be a kitty or a puppy. It's probably not a cookie. And it's not heavy enough to be a book."

Still holding the box, she looked at the floor with her sad face and said, "I hope it's not PJs. Mommy gives me PJs on Christmas Eve, and they are not very fun!"

Laughing, her father said, "Why don't you just open it? Do you need help?"

"NO!" cried Belinda! "I can do it by myself!" And pulling the pretty ribbon, she quickly opened the box and found something that was definitely NOT PJs or a kitty or a puppy or even a cookie.

"OH MY OH MY OH MY," Belinda whispered, reaching carefully into the box and taking out her present.

Holding it as if it might break, she showed her father, saying, "This is the most beautifulest dress ever in the whole world. Are you sure this is for ME? I have dresses for church, but not like THIS!"

"Well," her father said, "the box was addressed to you, and it was sent by Grandmother. So I am quite sure that it's for you. In fact, the green of your beautiful dress is the same color as your eyes, and that will make it really pretty when you wear it."

Running to a mirror, Belinda held the beautiful dress in front of her, squinting at her face to see if her eyes were really as green as the dress.

Turning around and around, she said, "Maybe I'll draw a picture of my First Present on my Advent Calendar! It will be SO be-yoo-tee-full!!"

When it was bedtime that day, Belinda's father hung the First Present of Christmas right on the door of Belinda's closet. She would be able to see it first thing in the morning, when she opened her eyes. She tried to keep her eyes open for a long time, staring at the dress until her eyes got very, very… heavy…

December 4: Inside the Box

What do you think Belinda will do first when she wakes up today? Last night, her eyes got so tired from looking at her new dress that she just... fell...asleep! Do you think she will want to make sure that her special present is still hanging on the closet door? Let's see!

"Good morning, Howard," whispered Belinda. "I want to whisper a little bit because I am so happy that I don't even want to get up yet."

Lying very still, she curled her toes and stared at her closet. "Howard, I was wondering if You saw my present from Grandmother? Even though I talk to You every day, I wondered if You are ever busy somewhere else? SO I will tell You ALL about my present, just in case!!"

Flopping over on her bed, she continued. "When Dad got the box out of the closet yesterday, I knew it was too big to be a book or a cookie, so I had to shake it just a little bit. It made a little soft noise, but it wasn't very heavy. So I shook it a little more!"

Shaking her head, the little girl continued. "I had some trouble with the pretty ribbon, but Dad helped me. And he said I didn't have to worry about breaking it. Then we put the box on the table so I could open it."

"I could hardly believe it was for me, and I rubbed my hand over it. It felt so soft! I even asked my dad if he was sure it was for me, and he said it was."

Opening her eyes at last, Belinda focused like a laser on the dress that hung on her closet door. "Oh, Howard," she gasped, "I know that my new dress is not what makes it Christmas, but it reminds me of Christmas because it's the color of a Christmas tree. BUT instead of being stickly and prickly like a tree, it's soft like Custard's fur. I love the big green velvet sash and the long green sleeves. Daddy said the dress was the same color as my eyes, and that would make it extra pretty when I wear it FOR REAL."

Sighing, she curled her toes and said, "Thank You for the dress and thank You for Grandmother and thank You for my warm bed and even thank You for Custard."

Jumping out of bed she remembered that her father said there was a STORY about the dress, and she could hardly wait to get downstairs and hear the story!

Racing down the stairs, she tripped just a little, in her excitement.

She managed to recover quickly and remind her father, "The story, the story, the story! Was it a fairy princess dress? Did it have magical powers? And how did Grandmother know that I would love this dress so much?"

Sam rolled his eyes at Gramps when he heard Belinda's questions coming in threes, as usual. "Must be showtime," he said, reaching into the pocket of his jeans and pulling out a letter. "How about if I tell you the story while we have breakfast?"

"Is that the story? Is it in the letter? Is it from Grandmother?" Belinda asked.

"Yes, yes, and yes," her father laughed.

Belinda looked over her father's shoulder at her grandmother's letter and said, "I think you'd better read it. I'm a good reader, but Grandmother's writing is pretty squiggly!"

Laughing, her father said, "Yes, you are a good reader, but these squiggles are even a challenge for me." Putting on his glasses, he read,

Dear Belinda,

Now that you are six years old, it's time to start doing some of the things I did long ago when I was six years old. I know you won't believe that I was EVER six years old, but it's true.

By now you know about the dress I sent you, but you don't yet know that it's for a very special occasion. You are going to take the train to see me in New York City, and you will wear your new dress to attend The Nutcracker Ballet. If your mother gets home in time, she will come too. And the three of us will do this every

Christmas as I did with my mother and grandmother when I was a little girl.

I am excited about your visit to New York and look forward to seeing you in your new dress.

Love,

Grandmother

Counting on her fingers, Belinda made sure she had the whole story: "FIRST we are going to New York to visit Grandmother, and SECOND I am going to wear my new dress, and THIRD we are going to The Nutcracker?"

"Yes," her father laughed. "And isn't it funny that Grandmother sent you a present in THREEs? I guess she must know you pretty well!"

"Couldn't we go right now?" asked Belinda, dancing around the kitchen in her best ballet twirls. "I could be ready in just the fastest minute!"

"I'm sure you could," her father said, pouring oatmeal and blueberries into a bowl for Belinda. "But you have to go to school today, and tonight we have to work on your Advent Calendar. When we have a spare minute, I'll tell you all about the plan for your trip, so eat up your oatmeal. You'll need plenty of energy with so many things to do!"

"I hate waiting," Belinda grumbled, sneaking a small blob of oatmeal to the floor for Custard. "I don't know how you can wait extra fast, but I'll work on it today and maybe the SPECIAL PLAN will come faster. I hope! AND I'm going to try to draw a picture of my Nutcracker dress on the Advent Calendar!"

December 5: Making Cookies

Belinda's Advent Calendar is starting to fill up. It now includes a drawing of her mom with soldiers and a Christmas tree. And now a drawing of her Nutcracker dress. Hmm. Do you think she's on the right track for "What is it that makes it Christmas?" Do you think she's missing something?

"Geez, Custard," Belinda growled. "Could you just not step on my head when I'm not even awake yet? You make my hair stick out like… like…like…porcupine quills!"

Custard's small paws hit the floor with a thump.

"That's not much of an answer," she grumbled as she scrunched down into her warm bed.

One rollover and a foot wiggle later, she realized that she was awake and ready to start the day: Maybe it was that cat footprint on her head!

"Good morning, Howard!" she said aloud. "It's a good thing I love that kitty a lot or I'd be very mad this morning." Giggling, she continued, "But some kids aren't lucky enough to have a cat like Custard, so I guess a few paw prints on my head are okay."

Sitting up in bed, she peeked at the calendar on her wall and remembered that today was a half day at school. OH BOY!

Barely able to get her robe on right side out, she raced into the kitchen to find out what she would be doing in the afternoon.

"Good morning, Dad," Belinda said. "It's a half day of school today, so are we going to make cookies or shop for presents or make decorations or…"

"Slow down, Belinda," her father laughed. "You already have three questions out there! And I thought it would be a great afternoon to make cookies."

"Super, awesome, hot, hot, hot!" said Belinda.

"I guess that's a yes," her grandfather said.

"What kind of cookies? I like cookies with green sprinkles like Christmas trees, and I like chocolate chip cookies when they are still gooey. But my FAVORITE is the kind we made last year that I can stick my finger in!"

"Oh, you mean thumbprint cookies," her father said.

"YES," roared Belinda in her outside voice as she danced around the kitchen, careful not to step on the cat.

"We put thumbs in and then we put jam in and then we asked Mommy if she could tell which ones were yours and which ones were mine AND I wanted to have paw print cookies made by Custard!"

"You must have had fun last year if you remember it so well! Let's start with thumbprint cookies and Christmas tree cookies and do chocolate chips another day. How does that sound?"

"PERFECT," came another roar from Belinda as she raced to the table to eat her breakfast.

That afternoon, Belinda and her father put on big aprons and turned on the oven. They began stirring and mixing (and tasting!) the batter for the first batch of cookies. Belinda liked to lick the beaters while her father put the trays of cookies in the oven.

"Licking beaters is almost as good as eating cookies," she said, licking the last of the dough off her lips.

Looking at her father with a serious, dough-covered face, Belinda said, "Good thing Mom wasn't here! She doesn't like me to lick the beaters. She says the eggs in the dough have not been cooked yet and could make me sick." Raising her eyebrows at her dad, who had allowed her this special pleasure, she said, "I won't tell if you don't!" Her father raised his eyebrows, looking innocent.

Soon Belinda was twitching her nose, enjoying the good smells from the oven, as Custard nestled peacefully in the windowsill.

"Custard," Belinda said, turning to look at her kitty in the windowsill, "you are a big faker. I know that you are awake and just waiting for cookies. But ALL of these cookies are for people. They are not for cats. Do you understand?" Only soft snuffles came from the windowsill as Custard pretended to be asleep. And even his wiggly tail was still.

"A peaceful moment for a change!" Belinda's father murmured. And no sooner had the words crossed his lips than Custard leapt oh-so-quietly onto the floor from the windowsill. "Uh-oh," he said. "Why do I have a feeling that that cat is up to no good?"

While peeking in the oven as the next batch of cookies baked, Belinda didn't hear her father or the soft sound of Custard's paws. By the time she turned around, she was just in time to see Custard streaking away. His whiskers were frosted with cookie, a huge kitty cat smile of contentment stretching from ear to ear. Belinda tried to catch up with him, but he was not only fast—he was sneaky!

Returning to the kitchen, Belinda said, "Oh that Custard! I knew he was looking at our cookies the way he looks at his dinner." After pausing a moment, she continued. "BUT they are awfully good, and he only took one, so it's okay with me if it's okay with you."

Her father laughed and wondered aloud what they could do about it at that point anyway, since the cookie was now a part of Custard.

Laughing together at that naughty cat, Belinda and her father heard the sound of boots coming up the walk to the house. Soon Belinda's grandfather strode into the kitchen, taking off his heavy coat and hanging up his hat as he came.

"I love that hat, Gramps! It always makes me giggle," Belinda said.

"You mean the one that says, 'Your dog ate what???'"

"Yes," Belinda giggled again. "I guess it's a vet-er-in-ar-i-an joke!"

"What did I miss?" Gramps asked as he took off his boots.

"Oh, Gramps," Belinda said, "I'm not sure I should tell you. Custard took one of our cookies and ran to his basket, his whiskers all covered with cookie."

"Hmmm," her grandfather said as he chose two cookies from the table. "Here's a big cookie with a little print and here's a little cookie with a big print. Choosing the right one isn't going to be easy," he said as he munched the cookies.

"Oh, Gramps," Belinda laughed. "You did that so Daddy wouldn't notice that you ate more cookies than Custard. You're a big cookie thief too!"

"Shhh," said her grandfather. "Pretty soon your father will know all my secrets, and then where will we be?"

Smiling, Belinda said, "I know where I will be when we are finished baking cookies. I will be at the kitchen table trying to decide what to draw on my Advent Calendar today! I think maybe cookies and cat whiskers!"

Her father chuckled, saying, "I can't wait to see that one!"

December 6:
A Snowy Day for Decorating

Do you ever feel extra cold when you wake up in the morning? Belinda has a kitty, but sometimes even a kitty is not enough to keep you warm on a chilly morning! Especially if you live near 1234 Old River Road!

"Mumph! I must have pushed the covers off in my sleep," Belinda mumbled, still only half awake. Brrrr! Climbing back under the warm covers, she slid down in her bed until only her nose stuck out.

After she was warm again, she wondered why it felt even colder than usual, and why the light in her room was kind of gray and funny. Even though she was very cold, she tiptoed across the room and peeked out the window. Her eyes widened with excitement when she saw that the ground was covered with snow. "No wonder it was so quiet and cold and odd. That explains it," she said to herself.

"Howard," whispered Belinda, her warm breath fogging the window. "Look—it's snow! Oh boy, it's snow! Thank You very much for beautiful snow!"

Custard rolled over in the warm bed and looked at Belinda with one eye open. Stretching and yawning, he let her know that snow was not all that big a deal in his eyes.

Tucking Custard under one arm, Belinda pulled on her warm robe and bedroom slippers and made it to the top of the stairs but stopped when she heard her grandfather speaking very softly, like maybe he was saying something she wasn't supposed to hear.

"I'll bet Belinda will be excited that it's snowing," Gramps said. Then he stopped for a moment and whispered, "You know, I think I'm going to plan something special for all of us to do."

"You mean you're not even going to tell me?" asked Belinda's father.

"No," Gramps said with a chuckle, "I'm not."

Well, as you can imagine, Belinda couldn't stay put another minute. She tightened her grip on Custard, and when her dad and grandfather turned around, they saw Belinda and Custard practically flying toward them.

"What is the surprise? What is it, what is it?" Belinda wanted to know.

"Good morning, Belinda!" her father said. "Did you forget something?"

“Oh no,” said Belinda as her face stretched into her biggest “Belinda the Grown-Up Actress” smile. “Good mor-ning to Dad-dy and Gramps from Belinda and Cust-ard,” she said in a singsong voice.

Back to her question, she demanded, “NOW will you tell me what the surprise is?”

“Well, Belinda,” said her grandfather, “the snow gave me an idea for a special surprise, but I can’t tell you about it just yet.”

“Is it a PRESENT?” asked Belinda.

Gramps chuckled and said, “That depends on what you call presents.”

“Well,” said Belinda’s father. “I have a surprise for you right this minute. There will be no school today because of the snow, so we will all be at home. And Gramps thought you might like to help him start putting up lights outside to get our house ready for Christmas. What do you think?”

“What you can’t do,” said Belinda’s grandfather, “is bring that fool cat into the act. Can you imagine what he could do with a string of Christmas lights? We could end up with an electric cat!”

“Oh, Gramps,” Belinda laughed. “You’re right about that. I’ll make sure he stays out of our way the whole time, until we are all finished. BUT,” she snickered, “I can’t wait to see what happens when there are decorations everywhere.”

Each year, Belinda’s family had to think hard to remember whose turn it was to be in charge of lights and decorations. Belinda’s father and grandfather liked lots of colors—bright reds and blues and greens. Belinda’s mother liked pure white lights on the bushes and a single color on the tree. Belinda's grandfather loved lights that twinkled and blinked, and Belinda's mother liked the steady glow of untwinkly lights.

So every year, they took turns. One year, Belinda's father and grandfather had the outside lights just the way they liked them, and the house looked like a coloring book after a crayon explosion. Inside, Belinda's mother would do things her way, and the following year they would trade.

Belinda liked both ways and had her own ideas as well. She liked the lights okay, but what she liked best was making special decorations for the outdoor trees. "Gramps," she said as she began pulling on her boots, "when we're finished, I want to make some popcorn strings for the birds and hang up some fresh oranges. Birds like my ornaments even better than the lights, and I can stand inside to watch them WHIZ up to the tree to eat them!"

Smiling, Gramps carried boxes of lights from the garage to the front porch, promising to help with the popcorn strings and oranges once they finished with the lights.

Belinda's job was to test strings of lights, plugging each string into an outlet on the porch.

Then Gramps had to shake the snow off each of the bushes, so that he could thread the lights through each and every one.

"So far so good, Gramps," she said, as she carefully piled light strings on the porch ready for decorating.

"Wait a minute," Belinda said. "What do you do if none of the lights work? Do you just throw them away?"

"No," Gramps said. "Sometimes just one bulb is loose and makes the whole string stop working. But set those aside. They are probably old strings. The new ones work better—they keep working even if one bulb fails, and we try to get a few more of the new ones every year."

"Humph," said Belinda, as she plugged in another dead string of lights and tried wiggling some bulbs. "I hope we don't have a LOT of these lazy strings! We need to have PLENTY of lights for our house!"

Watching each string light up and handing it to Gramps to thread through the pretty evergreen bushes kept her busy for quite a long time. But eventually it was time for Belinda to run inside and turn on the switch, turning ordinary bushes and trees into fairyland, magical and bright with light.

Belinda hugged her grandfather and said, "Gramps, I'm going to draw a special picture of our house on my Advent Calendar tonight and it will be SUPER GREAT with LIGHTS and SNOW and popcorn strings and oranges!! I'll bet my mom will like it a lot, even if that's not what makes it Christmas."

"I'm sure she will," said Gramps. "I'm sure she will."

December 7: At the Tree Farm

Does your family put up a Christmas tree? Some families have to have a very small tree, and some families can't have a "real live" tree because someone in the family has "allergies." That means that the tree might make them cough or sneeze and feel all drippy at Christmas.

Belinda is lucky that no one in her family has allergies, and there is plenty of room at 1234 Old River Road for a BIG Christmas tree! Do you think she might be a LITTLE bit excited about a Christmas tree?

Belinda peeked at her calendar out of the corner of her eye and saw the red X she had drawn on each of the first six days of December. "Oh hot dog!!" she said. "It's SATURDAY!"

With her hands clasped, she looked to the sky with her most innocent expression, saying, "Thank You, Howard, for Saturday! Gramps promised that we would go to the tree farm today and pick out our Christmas tree. Oh super, super, Saturday!"

With that, she flew out the door to the kitchen.

Her father looked up to see another case of the Flying Belinda.

"Good morning, Belinda," her father said, catching her with one arm while flipping over an apple pancake with the other. "Are you feeling extra cheerful this morning?"

"Tree, tree, tree, Dad," said Belinda. "Today is the day we go to Mr. Corson's tree farm and pick our Christmas tree. Gramps said so. Right?"

"Do I smell apple pancakes?" Gramps asked as he took off his boots and hung up his coat and his funny hat. "And yes, Belinda, I said we would go today, and we will. As soon as we finish ALL of those apple pancakes your dad made for us."

Belinda's father put Belinda down and helped her cut her pancakes. "You remember that we are just going to look. We can pick our tree now, but it has to stay out in the cold until a few days before Christmas, and then we can go pick it up."

Fidgeting in her chair, Belinda asked, "Are you SURE we have to eat breakfast first? Can't we go right now? And can Custard come too?"

"Taking your questions in order, said her grandfather, "yes, we have to eat breakfast first. No, we can't go right now. And no, Custard can't come."

"All right," said Belinda, gulping down her breakfast and leaping up from the table. "Okay, okay! I will be READY in just one minute!"

Racing to the closet, Belinda grabbed her boots, jacket, mittens, scarf, and hat, putting them on as she hurried back to her place at the table.

Stuffing her mouth with the remains of her pancakes, Belinda tugged her boots on and zipped her parka at the same time. Chewing yet another bite, she wrapped her scarf around her neck, stuck her nose out, and mumbled through the woolly scarf, "NOW am I ready?"

Her father laughed so hard that Gramps grabbed his camera and took a quick picture of Belinda bundled in her snowflake jacket, red boots, scarf, mittens—and holding a fork!

"You look like a stuffed goose, with those fat cheeks full of pancakes!" Gramps said. "We'll send that picture to your mom as soon as we get back."

"OH!" said Belinda. "I will make her laugh even when she's far away!" She giggled as she thought about telling Elizabeth the story of a stuffed goose at breakfast!

While Gramps and her father put the breakfast dishes in the dishwasher, Belinda scribbled something on a piece of paper.

Carrying her scribbled piece of paper, she jumped into the truck with Gramps and her dad, singing "Jingle Bells" and bouncing as high as she could with excitement.

Driving down the country road to the tree farm, Belinda looked all around her. Then looked down at the paper she'd brought. "Oh no," she said softly. "I think I'm in big trouble!"

Her father helped her jump out of the truck, while Belinda shook her head and looked around some more.

"What's wrong, Belinda?" asked Gramps. "You've been waiting to get here, and now you look like you lost your Christmas list!"

"It's LIKE a Christmas list, Gramps," said Belinda. "While you and my dad were cleaning up the dishes, I made a list of what kind of tree I wanted to find. And I wrote it all down. See: I want a tree that's BIG and FAT and TALL and FRIENDLY!"

"That sounds like a great list to me," said Gramps. "So what's the problem?

"Did you LOOK at these trees, Gramps?" she said, spinning around in a circle. "ALL, ALL, ALL of the trees are BIG and FAT and TALL and FRIENDLY." Looking at him, nose to nose, she said, "So HOW will we ever pick just one?"

Just then a bright blue hat caught Belinda's attention. She recognized her friend, Elizabeth, who had a bright blue hat exactly like that.

"Oh, look, I see my friend Elizabeth! We can help each other find the best trees for our families!"

While racing off to Elizabeth without waiting for permission, Belinda felt her dad's strong hand on her shoulder. She looked up into his most serious face. "Belinda," her dad said, "you know that you are not supposed to just run off by yourself, even to see a friend. Do you remember why we have that rule?"

Sighing, Belinda looked down. She was sorry that she had forgotten an important rule on such a special day. "I can't just run off because I could get lost. Or a car could run over me in the street. Or my dad and gramps might be very worried. Or a bad stranger might talk to me."

"That's right," her father said. He didn't want to turn a happy day into a sad one, but he had to be sure Belinda would be safe. A quick conversation with Elizabeth's parents and the tree farm employees reassured him that the girls could wander safely.

"Whew," whispered Belinda to Elizabeth, "glad that's over! I thought I'd be in trouble all day instead of looking for trees!"

Elizabeth had a face as soft as chocolate ice cream and crinkly black hair with a million barrettes. She smiled at Belinda and took Belinda's freckly white hand in her soft brown one. The two girls skipped down a row of trees looking in every direction. Belinda pulled out her list from time to time to see if a particular tree passed the BIG and TALL and FAT and FRIENDLY test.

"Did you find your tree yet, Elizabeth?" Belinda asked. "Or are you still looking, like me?"

"No," said Elizabeth. "And I don't know how we will decide. Mom likes one kind, Dad likes another kind, and my brother likes a third kind. Maybe I should get the final vote?"

As Elizabeth checked out the trees all around them, she waved to her mom who was just a few trees away. "Still looking," Elizabeth said.

"Me too," Belinda whispered. "BUT I have a plan!"

"You do? What's your plan?"

"Well," Belinda said, "there are so many great trees. I will need a way to remember the very best ones." Belinda took off one of her red mittens and placed it on a branch of a particularly special tree. "See," she said, "this is a very good tree. With my mitten on the branch, I will be able to find it again to show Gramps and my dad!"

Elizabeth giggled. "The branch looks like a hand with a mitten! Good thing you have two mittens, a scarf, and a hat! I hope you're not thinking of putting your boots on a Christmas tree!"

Belinda looked down at her red boots and laughed. "Nah. But what are we going to do about YOUR tree?"

"I wouldn't want to put my blue hat on a tree," said Elizabeth. "I like it a way lot. My hair is so frizzy that Mom puts lots of little braids and b'rettes in it. My blue hat fits JUST RIGHT over top. But I could put mittens and a scarf on a tree. Let's go!"

It wasn't easy, but soon Belinda and Elizabeth had placed mittens, scarves, and Belinda's hat on seven different trees (four for Belinda and three for Elizabeth). Both girls were laughing as they ran to Belinda's father and Elizabeth's parents.

"We did it, we did it, we did it!!" Belinda crowed. "I found four trees and Elizabeth found three! So now we'll have to look at ALL of them, so Elizabeth and I can get our mittens and scarves and my hat back!"

Belinda took her father's hand in her cold one and tugged him down the row of trees to see a tree with a red mitten sticking out. "See?" asked Belinda. "We marked the spot, like a treasure map!"

"Well," said her father. "This is a very fine tree, but let's see the others before we decide."

Once the parents knew what the girls' "Treasure Map" would look like, they all set out to visit the trees and find the perfect one for each family.

Belinda's father pulled his warm winter hat down to cover his ears and pushed his glasses back up his nose. His bright red hat said "P," which Belinda thought was very funny. She thought it was a potty joke, but her dad said it was really about his school, the University of Pennsylvania.

By the time they had collected mittens, scarves, and one rather frozen red hat, everyone had agreed on trees that might not be perfect but were perfect for them.

It was time to get warm and celebrate!

"Hot chocolate!" pleaded Belinda. "When we came here last year, we got hot chocolate with whipped cream on top!"

"Ooooh," that sounds yum," said Elizabeth, looking up at her mother.

"I think it sounds yum myself," said Elizabeth's mother. She was a pretty woman with soft brown skin, friendly brown eyes, and black hair. "Even in my warm sweatshirt and parka, I'm a little bit cold! How about if Gramps and I go pay for the trees and make sure they put the right name on the right tree? And the rest of you can order hot chocolate for everyone?"

Just a few minutes later, Belinda wiggled her whipped cream mustache at Elizabeth and said, "I don't know how Christmas can get much better than this." With a devilish grin she continued, "But I'm ready to find out!"

When they got home, Belinda talked to her mother on Skype about the trip to the tree farm.

"Mommy," she said, "there were trees and trees and trees. Fat and skinny and tall and stubby. And big round ones all uneven, and sticky prickly ones. SO, I was thinking, that I wished we could take all of them home with us, and I was afraid some trees would be disappointed if we didn't pick them. BUT—remember what I did when I really, really liked a tree?"

"Of course I remember," said her mother. "You made sure that Gramps and I would come and look at your favorites, so you put a mitten on one, a scarf or hat on another. Lucky for us, you didn't put your boots or your snowflake jacket on a tree!"

Sipping her coffee, Belinda's mother said, "Oh! I'll bet I am guessing what you are going to draw for your dad."

"Yes, yes, yes," said Belinda. "A picture of four trees wearing red mittens and a scarf and a hat and you and Gramps too. Daddy will be wearing his P hat, and Gramps will be wearing his funny hat, and I will be wearing my snowflake jacket!"

"Pretty clever," her father chuckled. "You found a way to help us find the very best tree for our house."

"And," asked Belinda, "do you remember Clarence?"

"Of course," her mother said. "It's the first time you ever named a Christmas tree, so that had to be the one!"

“Yes,” said Belinda. “It was fat and friendly and just a little crooked, which I liked very much.”

“And so this year you found a tree named Clarence too, I’ll bet!” her mother said.

“YES!” said Belinda. And they waved and kissed good night with happy smiles, thinking of another special Christmas tree that would soon be coming to their house.

December 8: Church

Since yesterday was Saturday, today must definitely be SUNDAY. What do you and your family usually do on Sunday? Some people go to church. Some have a special dinner at Grandmother's house. Some go shopping or work on Christmas presents. I wonder what Belinda does on Sunday. Let's find out!

"Good morning, Howard," Belinda mumbled into her pillow. "Thank You for fun at the tree farm yesterday. I had a super time and can't wait to go back and get our tree and bring it right in our living room."

Burying her face deeper in her pillow, she said, "Howard, I have to stand up at church today with my VERY TALL Gramps and my VERY

TALL dad. I know it's an honor, but I kind of wish they would honor someone else! I like the singing part, but I have to say some stuff before we get to sing. I think I might feel just a little bit shrimpy for the talking part!"

Shaking her head, she said, "Okay, Howard, You probably can't make me bigger in one day, but please help me do a good job. And I hope YOU have a super great day Your Own Self!"

When Belinda walked slowly into the kitchen, whispering to herself, her father knew something must be wrong. Belinda didn't usually just WALK into the kitchen in the morning—she EXPLODED.

"Good morning, Belinda," her father said. "Are you practicing a Christmas carol?"

"No," Belinda whispered. "I'm practicing what I'm supposed to say at church. I asked Howard for help, but I REALLY want to get it right myself. Howard shouldn't have to do all the work!"

Chuckling, her father dropped more pancake batter onto the griddle. He turned to smile at his daughter. "You are a pretty smart kid! Some people dump everything on Howard and others forget to even ask Him for help. You did both—ask for help and try to do your best. How about if we practice while we have breakfast?"

By the time they were in their front-row seats at church, Belinda was not worried anymore. "How are you doing there, kiddo?" asked her father.

"I am READY!" she whispered in her best inside voice.

When they were called to the Advent Wreath, she walked with confidence holding hands with her father and her grandfather.

Everybody was so dressed up. Gramps was even wearing a tie, and he left his funny hat at home!

Her father picked up the giant candle lighter, and they took their places around the wreath.

Gramps pushed his glasses up his nose and looked down at Belinda and looked very serious. He said, “This is the second Sunday in Advent. Do you remember why we are taking time to be together in this circle around our Advent Wreath?”

Taking a deep breath, Belinda said, “We light a candle every week to remember that Advent is a time when we get our hearts ready for the coming of the Baby Jesus.”

Using the giant candle lighter thing-y, Belinda’s dad said: “I light this candle on the second Sunday in Advent. It is to remind us that Jesus came to earth to ‘show and tell’ us about God’s love.”

Whew! Belinda thought. We all got it right!

Safely back in her seat, Belinda sang with her best loud voice. Her dad turned to wink at her, proud that she had done something even though it was hard.

That night, Belinda told Custard all about it, and Custard looked at her with his best attention. “And,” said Belinda, “Pastor John smiled right at ME, and then we sang “Away in a Manger” and it was awesome! And people came up after church and said what a good job we did. My friend Elizabeth gave me a big hug, and Andrew said he thought I looked very brave!”

Pulling out her Advent Calendar, she began drawing a picture of an Advent wreath with three people around it—two very tall and one not so tall. "Whew," she said to Custard, "that's an awful lot to draw in one little box!"

When her dad came in to say good night, he overheard what she had told Custard. He said, "You can draw a BIG picture or a very small one. But the drawing will help you to remember what a great job you did today."

"Yes," Belinda nodded, chewing on her lip as she put the finishing touches on her drawing.

Before she nodded off to sleep, Belinda remembered to say thank you to Howard.

"Howard," she said, "thank You for helping me to get the words right. And my picture will help me to remember being with my dad and Gramps and lighting the Advent Wreath."

Looking across the room at her Advent Calendar, she said, "G'night, Howard. I love You and I can't wait to see what we're going to do tomorrow to get ready for Baby Jesus!"

And as Belinda relaxed into sleep, even Custard curled up and snoozed his quiet snooze.

December 9: Where Are You, Custard?

Uh-oh. We are not going to hear from Belinda until after school today! Something important is happening. Let's listen!

"Howard," whispered Belinda as she took off her boots in the mud room after school, "I know I talked to You this morning, but I need some extra time today. I am late getting home from school today, and Gramps says that Custard has been outside a long time. I hope he isn't too cold. I think I'll go check outside again and just call him one more time."

Belinda went to the door to see if Custard was ready to come back in. "Custard," she called. "Where are you, Custard?" But no little kitty cat answered.

Closing the door, Belinda went back in the house and plopped down at the kitchen table for maybe one minute.

Poking her nose into her dad's office, she said, "Daddy, Custard's been gone a very long time. And it's cold outside and there's snow on the ground. I think we should go look for him right away!"

"Well, Belinda," said her dad, "Custard has a nice warm coat and can stay outside for a long time without a problem. Let's wait just a little bit longer. Then, if he still hasn't come back, you and I will go looking for him. He may be in the garage, you know, under one of the cars. Or up in a tree. Or visiting a neighbor. You know how clever Custard is. He could be sitting in a neighbor's kitchen this very moment, having a nice saucer of milk before he comes home."

Wrinkling her forehead, Belinda said, "Oh, Daddy, I hope so. But I wish he would come home. Can we do something while we wait? 'Cause my feet have the jumpy jitters, and I can't sit very still if I don't know where Custard is."

"What would you like to do, Belinda?" asked her father. He closed his laptop and walked toward the kitchen. "Shall we play a game or read a story or eat some of our nice, fresh chocolate chip cookies? What would help to make the jumpy jitters go away, do you think?"

Munching a cookie, Belinda said, "You are a very good story reader, but I think we need to do something very noisy, because it's so quiet. I keep thinking I hear Custard's little paws on the porch, when he isn't out there at all."

"Hmmm," said her father. "I think I know just the thing." And off he went to put on some Christmas music—and VERY LOUD indeed.

"Is that better, Belinda?" he shouted, so Belinda could hear him over the music.

"That is wonderful, Daddy," shouted Belinda. "And what are we going to do now, while the music plays?"

Taking Belinda's hand, her dad said, "How about if we dance to the music? You can spin and twirl and pretend you are a real ballerina, like we see on TV?"

"Oh YES," said Belinda, clasping both of her father's hands. They laughed and spun their way around furniture, till they finally plopped down on chairs, exhausted from laughing so hard.

"Well," said Belinda, "that made me think about something besides Custard for a while.

"Oh," Belinda's dad said. "That's my phone, and I wouldn't have heard it ringing if we were still dancing to the music!"

"Hello," he said.

"Sam," a worried voice said, "is Elizabeth at your house, playing with Belinda? She went out sledding a little while ago, and I told her to be home before dark. But she isn't here yet."

Walking into the next room with the phone, Sam said, "No, Nancy, we haven't seen Elizabeth this afternoon. We were thinking about going out to look for Custard, because he's been gone for a long time. Sounds like we need a plan for finding both of them. Do you know what color hat and coat Elizabeth was wearing? That might help the searchers. Have you called the police or other friends? Are there people you would like me to call while you search?"

Sam had been speaking very softly, but Belinda had poked her head around the corner to listen, just in case the call was about Custard. Instead of being GOOD news, the call made things even worse. Elizabeth was missing TOO?

As he got off the phone, Belinda's father saw the worry in his daughter's wide green eyes. Even her freckles had lost their color.

"It's okay, Belinda, we're on it. You and I and lots of other people are going to get to work to find Custard AND Elizabeth. Can you help me right away?"

Nodding like a bobblehead, she said, "Where do we start? I'm ready to get to work!"

"First," her father said, seating her at the kitchen table with a pencil and paper, "I want you to make a list of Elizabeth's friends. We're going to call them and see if maybe Elizabeth got very cold and went to the nearest house to get warm."

"Okay!" said Belinda, who never needed to be told twice when there was important work to do.

Belinda finished her list and gave it to her father. He began making phone calls while they bundled up in their warmest clothes. Belinda's dad checked that her boots were snug and her scarf tucked in before heading out to look for Custard and Elizabeth.

Trying not to shiver, Belinda kept her eyes on the ground. She looked for a paw print or the print of a little girl's boot. But the snow had covered everything, and there was nothing to see. Looking around she called out, "CUSTARD! ELIZABETH! WHERE ARE YOU?" But the only answer was the soft fall of even more snow.

They climbed into the truck that sat up high so they could see better.

"Okay, Belinda," her father said as he watched her look out the window. "We've called friends and neighbors and the SPCA and even the police. But no one has seen Custard or Elizabeth. So we are going to drive all around town and especially near Elizabeth's house. I am counting on you to look for anything that looks like Elizabeth or Custard. She's wearing her blue coat and hat. Those bright colors might help!"

"I'll be looking too, but I have to pay attention to the road when I'm driving."

Soon Belinda and her father saw other people searching too. Some had their heads out the window calling for Elizabeth and Custard.

After a very long search, they returned home again, with no kitty in sight. Belinda was so sad she sat on the floor in a corner, and tiny tears slid down her cold cheeks, thinking about her friend and her kitty. She liked having exciting days and Christmas surprises, but she wasn't going to draw THIS day on her Advent calendar. It was too scary!

"Time to talk to Howard," she thought as she climbed into her father's lap, worn out from all the worries.

In her quietest voice, she whispered, "Howard, I know that lots of days I only talk to you in the morning because I get very busy. And I already asked You for help a little while ago because I was so worried about Custard. But it's later and darker and colder, and now I need to talk to You about my friend Elizabeth too!"

Belinda couldn't sit still, and she climbed down from her father's lap. She walked to the window yet again. Her eyes searched everywhere for Custard and Elizabeth. She looked up the apple tree, down the long driveway to the bright red mailbox, out on the road. Nothing.

"Howard," Belinda continued, "You know that Custard is a very small kitty and I love him very much, even when he gets into things. If he is with Elizabeth, could You help both of them come home safe and soon?"

Meanwhile, not very far away, Custard was having the most amazing adventure. He had chased two mice, scared some birds, gotten brambles in his coat, and climbed some scratchy trees. But now it was getting cold and very dark.

As he began making his way home, however, Custard put his nose to the ground, following a funny smell. It wasn't dog. And it wasn't squirrel. He moved carefully as he got closer to the smell, until he finally noticed that the funny smell smelled a little like Belinda! Twitching his nose, he went closer still. Whatever it was, it looked like a person, but it wasn't moving.

Like all of his cat ancestors, Custard knew how to sneak up on something, one quiet little paw at a time.

Turning his head in all directions, he moved even closer, then JUMPED up on the still little person who smelled like Belinda. Custard began licking the little person's face, since that usually convinced Belinda that it was time to play.

At that very moment, Custard looked up from face licking and heard a loud screech! He was frozen to the spot, staring into a set of car headlights. “What on earth is this?” the driver of the car said. “What is going on here?”

And with that, a small passenger with round glasses and a serious face unfastened his seat belt. He jumped out of the car, tripping over the pile of books between him and the door.

“Gramps,” said the little boy, “that’s Elizabeth from my school. She must have sledded down the big hill and onto the road. She’s hurt!”

“Yes, Andrew,” said his grandfather, pushing his glasses up his nose. Looking at his watch, he pushed up the sleeve of Elizabeth’s bright blue coat and took her wrist. “Her heart is beating just fine. It was incredibly lucky that that cat happened to be there. My headlights shone on his bright yellow eyes. Otherwise I would not have seen Elizabeth in the road until it was too late.”

Andrew loved that his grandfather always made him feel like everything was going to be okay—even when something scary happened. Like his friend Elizabeth almost getting run over!

While his grandfather reached for his phone to call 911 for help, Andrew looked up at him. His grandfather looked exactly like he always looked. He was a very tall schoolteacher, and everyone said he looked like a schoolteacher. He had gray hair and bushy eyebrows, and his glasses were silvery around the outside instead of brown.

When his grandfather finished calling 911, Andrew just couldn’t stop talking.

“Gramps,” Andrew said, “I recognize that kitty! It’s Belinda’s kitty, Custard. He must have gotten out and she will be so worried! I bet he recognized Elizabeth 'cause she is Belinda's best friend!"

Talking faster, he said, "I'm Elizabeth's friend too, but sometimes Belinda and Elizabeth tease me a little." He looked up at his grandfather and said, "Sometimes they call me Harry Potter, but they aren't mean. It's just 'cause I wear glasses like Harry. I call them Hermione!!"

Andrew reached down and picked up the kitty. Custard snuggled in his arms, enjoying the nice warm feeling.

Just then, Elizabeth stirred and moaned. "Mom," she whimpered. "I want my mom."

"Wake up, Elizabeth," Andrew's grandfather said in his softest voice. "You've had a bad spill but you're going to be okay now." And while his grandfather called Elizabeth's mother, Andrew hung onto Custard and held Elizabeth's hand at the same time. "Everything's going to be okay now, Elizabeth," Andrew said. "I promise!"

December 10: Custard Comes Home

Wow—I wanted Belinda to have an exciting day but not a scary one! It sounds like she doesn't know yet that everything is going to be okay! Have you ever worried about something—or someone—and it all turned out okay? Let's listen as Belinda finds out what her kitty has been doing out in the cold night!

As the cold winds blew, Andrew and his grandfather and Custard waited for Elizabeth's mom and an ambulance.

Soon Elizabeth and her mom were headed for the hospital to make sure Elizabeth was really ok. Sometimes a hit on the head has to be checked, and the doctors would do just that.

Meanwhile Andrew's grandfather drove straight to Belinda's house with Andrew and Custard in the back seat.

Belinda heard tires crunching on the driveway, and then, just a moment later, the doorbell rang. "Who can that be?" Belinda's father asked as he went to the door. "Maybe it's about Elizabeth and Custard!" cried Belinda.

"Oh, Belinda," said her dad as he peeked around the door. "These are visitors that you will be very, very glad to see." With that the door opened and Custard leaped out of Andrew's arms and straight into Belinda's.

"Custard!" Belinda shrieked. "You're back, you crazy kitty! But how did you end up with Andrew?" Shaking her head, Belinda carried a dirty and bedraggled Custard into the warm kitchen.

"Come in!" said Belinda's father to Andrew and his grandfather. "Thank you so much for bringing Custard home! Did you know that Elizabeth was missing too? She went sledding hours ago, and her mother said she had not come home yet. We were hoping she might be with Custard."

"Well," said Andrew's grandfather, "you can stop worrying about Elizabeth AND Custard." Glancing at his grandson, he said, "Would you like to tell the story of Custard the Hero or would you like me to tell it?"

"My Custard, a hero?" asked Belinda.

"Yes, Belinda," said Andrew. "And it's all true."

“Excuse me,” said Belinda’s father, “but before we hear the story, should we call Elizabeth’s mother?”

“It’s okay,” said Andrew’s grandfather. “I called her before we came here, but it’s quite a story.”

“In that case,” Belinda’s father said, “let’s sit down and have some hot chocolate! Andrew’s hands and face are red from the cold.”

“That’s very nice of you,” Andrew’s grandfather smiled. “Don’t mind if I do.”

Andrew and his grandfather took off their warm hats and jackets and boots, ready to sit down and have hot chocolate.

And as they sat around the farmhouse table with steamy mugs of hot chocolate warming their hands, the story of Custard the Hero was told, just as it was being told all over town that night. No one knew why Custard had been missing all day, and no one knew why he was out in the middle of a road. But what they did know was that maybe Custard was exactly where he was meant to be on that cold December night, licking the cold face of Belinda’s best friend.

In fact, Elizabeth’s mother believed it was a Christmas miracle. “Why,” she asked everyone, “would Belinda’s kitty find Elizabeth out in the road? And why would Custard lick Elizabeth’s face? AND why did Custard look up just in time for a driver to see his yellow eyes?

“If Custard hadn’t looked up,” she said, “it might have been too late for both of them. That sounds exactly like a miracle to me!”

Belinda held Custard close. She shivered at the thought of what could have happened to Elizabeth if it weren’t for Custard.

Belinda's eyes filled with tears and with pride. "Oh," she said to Andrew. "Thank goodness for Custard. And thank goodness it was you who found him. Someone else might never have brought him back to me!"

She stopped a moment, then asked, "But what about Elizabeth? Is she going to be okay?"

"She's going to be fine," Andrew's grandfather assured her. "She got a bad bump on the head that knocked her out, and we sent for an ambulance to take her to the hospital. But I've spoken with the doctors and they say she'll be just fine. All thanks to that kitty cat, Custard."

Andrew said, "When Elizabeth got to the hospital, people started telling the story all over the place. By now EVERYONE in town has heard about Custard the Hero. You can bet that Custard can have a saucer of milk and a place by the fire anywhere he wants! And Elizabeth's mom and dad are going to come and say thank you in person. They are so happy that she is going to be okay."

Belinda said to Andrew, "It's like a Christmas present! Custard doesn't have a ribbon or a bow, but he came home safe and sound. And Elizabeth is going to be okay. That's TWO presents."

Gramps commented, "Yes, Belinda, but you like things in threes. So what's the third present?"

Belinda thought a minute and said softly, "Feeling happy in my heart is a present. And that makes three."

Gramps smiled and said, "Indeed it does."

After all the goodbyes were said and Belinda's house settled into night, the little girl and her heroic kitty went off to bed. They were happy to be together again and ready to share their stories of the day where no one else could hear. With one arm around her kitty, Belinda remembered to say thank you to Howard. She fell asleep wondering if a happy heart with a cat inside might be what Christmas is all about.

December 11: Fun in the Snow

What a day Belinda and Custard had! She had a hard time staying still when she was worrying about Custard. I wonder if she will want to be outside doing fun things today now that her kitty is back home?

"Shhhh!" Belinda whispered to Custard. "Listen to how quiet it is this morning. Everybody must still be sleeping."

Still being very quiet, Belinda grabbed Custard and tucked him under the covers with her. After all the excitement of Custard being a hero, it was important that he keep her company for her morning talk with Howard.

“Howard,” Belinda said, trying to hold that wiggly kitty still, “I know that Custard would say thank You for bringing him home if he knew how to talk. But I’ll have to say it for both of us. THANK YOU, Howard, for the big, super, major present of getting my kitty back safely.” As Belinda kissed the top of Custard’s soft head, the little cat looked up at her and shook himself.

“I guess he had enough moosh,” Belinda giggled. “Custard is not very good at moosh. But I AM,” said Belinda, “and I would hug You, Howard, if I knew how. So I hope You have a special happy wonderful day today!”

With that, the little girl jumped out of bed and grabbed her robe and slippers, stopping at the window for a quick peek.

“Oh! How beautiful! It snowed AGAIN!”

Quiet as a mouse, Belinda tiptoed down the stairs and pulled her boots, parka, mittens, and scarf from the closet. She carried the red rubber boots to the back door, and she pulled on her parka and scarf as she went.

“Hard to tiptoe with boots on,” she said to herself as she closed the door. “Good thing I waited till I was almost outside. I’m not supposed to go outside without telling anyone, but sometimes the snow just calls my name!!”

Looking up at the still-falling snow, she stuck her tongue out and moved her head this way and that till she felt a cold snowflake on her warm tongue. Smiling with happiness, she picked up a fistful of snow and began rolling it into a small ball. When the snow started trickling through her cold, wet fingers, she laid the ball on the ground.

She rolled it around till it was a little bigger and a little bigger and a little bigger. Giggling with the effort, she kept pushing the ball around in all directions till it was big enough to make the base of a snowman. Resting a minute, she looked it over and nodded. "Looking good, Mr. Snowman," she whispered. "I'll bet the next part will be easier!"

And it was! She rolled another ball until it was just the right size for the snowman's middle. But when it was time to lift the snowman's middle, it wasn't so easy!

"Mr. Snowman," she panted, "you have a big belly and it's a little heavy for me!" Plopping it into place, she grinned and patted it. She scraped off some snow where the roundness was a little rounder than it should be.

Tilting her head to the side, she said, "Mr. Snowman, you are a little bit chubby but very friendly. I hope you will be okay till later because I'm going to need help to get your head on! I can make a GREAT head for you, but I don't think I can lift it unless Gramps lets me use a ladder! I'm going away now, but I'll be back!"

With one last glance at the snowman, she crept back into the house and took off her wet things. She whispered to herself, "Maybe Daddy and Gramps would like to come and see my headless snowman."

Sure enough, her father was already in the kitchen. "Belinda," he said, "your cheeks are awfully rosy this morning."

"Yes, Daddy," giggled Belinda. "And they're very cold besides!"

"Indeed they are," her father said as he hugged the little girl. "How come you are so cold?"

Belinda touched her rosy cheeks with cold fingers and laughed. "I have been outside already, working on a surprise for you and Gramps." And with that, she tugged her father toward the nearest window. "Look! I have made the world's first headless snowman!"

"Oh, Belinda," her dad said, with a serious face. "No wonder your face is so cold! You must have been out in the snow for a while. And did you ask Gramps about going outside? Because I know you didn't ask me."

Belinda looked down at her wet feet and shook her head. "No, Daddy. I didn't ask Gramps or you. It was so quiet, and I just knew it was time to make a snowman. I didn't want to have to wait and WASH MY HANDS and EAT BREAKFAST before I could go out. So…" Still looking at her feet, she said, "I am sorry that I went out without asking. But I hope you will still like my snowman!"

Sighing, her father lifted her chin and looked at her rosy cheeks. "I am glad you know that you weren't supposed to go out without letting us know. How about if we make a deal: The next time you have to go out in the snow immediately, you promise to come tell me, and I promise to let you go, even without breakfast. Is that a fair deal?"

Smiling up at her father, Belinda said, "That is a very fair deal. After breakfast, do we have time to finish the snowman before I have to go to school?"

"Hmmm," said her father. "Lucky for your snowman, school is closed because of the snow. So, I was thinking that we might have a play-at-home-day today and do some work on your Advent Calendar. We've been so busy keeping up with Custard's adventures that we haven't even had time to think about it."

“Gramps!” Belinda called as her grandfather came into the room. “I need your help today with my headless snowman!”

Chuckling at his granddaughter, Gramps followed Belinda to the window to check out the headless snowman.

“Well,” he said, “I heard your father say that school was closed again today. So I guess we will have plenty of time to give your snowman a head—AFTER breakfast.” Excited, Belinda ran for the coat closet.

“And by the way, Belinda,” her grandfather said, “that is a very fine snowman you made. It’s true that he needs a head, but the rest of him was well done. Good job!”

Skipping her way to the sink to wash her hands, Belinda said, “Thank you, Gramps! I think the snowman is excellent too, but it’s hard to give him a smile when he doesn’t have a head. So we’ll work on that later for sure!”

Belinda’s father was busy pouring juice and setting the table. He smiled at the happy conversation and updated Gramps on the rest of the plan for the morning.

“Well,” Belinda said, “my Advent Calendar is also not finished. But not headless.” (She giggled to herself at this idea.)

“Today we’re going to catch up on what we have so far and maybe even read some of your favorite Christmas books.”

“Okay,” said Belinda swallowing quickly so she wouldn’t talk with her mouth full of breakfast. “Let’s see: snowman and Advent Calendar and reading. That’s three. I like it!”

Gramps shook his head and laughed as Belinda ate her breakfast and reached for her crayons at the same time.

"What do you have on your Advent Calendar so far, Belinda?" he asked.

Tucking a bite of breakfast into her cheek like a chipmunk, Belinda said, "I have a tree with Mommy and soldiers. And a heart with Custard inside. And a present from Grandmother. I know that those things are not WHAT IT IS THAT MAKES IT CHRISTMAS, but maybe I can draw a picture of a snowman with a big smile!"

Looking at her father, Belinda said, "Did you know that there is something special about snowmen? I DO! You know why?"

As Belinda's father shrugged his shoulders, Belinda continued. "I know that I have never ever seen a snowman that was mean or angry or even sad. And maybe that's part of what Christmas is all about!"

"I think you may be onto something there, Belinda," said Gramps. "I'll bet your smiling snowman will be quite a picture."

December 12: Homemade Presents

Belinda has been so busy getting ready for Christmas and trying to figure out the answer to her mother's question, there's something she forgot to do! She never made a present for her parents!

Do you ever make a present for your mom or dad or brother or sister or grandmother or grandfather or aunt or uncle? Belinda REALLY likes to draw pictures for her parents. Let's see what she's doing today!

"Humph," Belinda mumbled into her pillow. She twitched her nose. "Custard," she said, you're awfully close to my face, you know."

Sticking her face out from under the covers, she eased the kitty onto the foot of her bed. She sat up in the quiet morning and looked around.

"Humph," Belinda said again. "Good morning, Howard! I think I need to talk to You about a couple things today. I've been having a really good time getting ready for Christmas, but I don't know if I'm doing what my mom asked me to do. SO if You could help me work on that today, I would like that a lot. When we sing Christmas carols, I always think about the Little Drummer Boy. He didn't have a present for Baby Jesus, so he brought all he had—his drum and his song. I wonder if maybe that is a clue?"

Rolling over in bed, she said, "ALSO, I forgot to ask about the secret PLAN Gramps mentioned. So maybe You could help me remember."

"AND one more thing: Would You please keep an eye on my mom? I miss her a lot and hope she will be able to come home soon. I try not to ask my dad too much because I know he misses my mom too. But we'll all feel better if we know You are keeping an eye on her."

Jumping out of bed, she shouted, "AMEN and HAVE A GREAT DAY!"

Breakfast with Belinda's dad and Gramps was great, as always. It wasn't time yet for Christmas vacation, but Belinda had BIG PLANS for after school today.

As soon as she got home, she put her parka and her mittens and her boots away. Of course, she also said hello to Custard and stopped in her dad's office to give him a quick hug.

"What are you up to today, Belinda? Any plans?" her father asked.

"Oh," she said. "Just a few things I need to do. Don't worry about me!"

Just then his phone rang, and he looked at her with a bit of an "uh-oh" look on his face. But by then she was gone.

Oh so quietly, Belinda and Custard climbed the stairs to the old, old attic at the top of the house. "Custard," whispered Belinda, "some kids don't have an attic in their house, but we do! Gramps has lived here for a LONG time and is VERY old, so I'll bet we can find some OLD stuff in the attic to make presents with!"

The attic had creaky floors and was kind of dusty and made Belinda sneeze. But she had a special plan in mind, and she needed some things from the attic to carry out her plan.

When she was talking to Howard that morning, Belinda had had a really good idea. She was going to plan a special surprise for her parents, to say I love you in a very special way. AND she wanted to make a present for Grandmother, to say thank you for the awesome new dress!

She might not have a drum or a song like the Little Drummer Boy, but she would make them a Christmas present that they would never forget. And the attic was the place to begin!

Carefully climbing down the old attic stairs, Belinda tiptoed into her room with her arms filled to the chin with old clothes. But not just any old clothes. She had found dresses with sequins and bows and feathers and sparklies. She whisked them through the door to her room just a tiny step after Custard's tail made it through.

Custard mewed his protest at the near escape. He then curled up in Belinda's "nest," a window seat of soft pillows and lumpy old stuffed animal friends. Meanwhile, Belinda carefully spread her treasures on the floor, a grown-up look of concentration on her face. "Hmmm, Custard," she said. "These presents are going to take a lot of work. And you have to stay out of it, or we'll have a picture of kitty cat glued to the paper."

Hands on her hips, Belinda gave a very firm look at her kitty. "Custard," she said slowly, "do I have to send you downstairs while I work on my presents?" Custard closed his eyes and yawned, a superior kitty cat look on his face.

"Oh, Custard," Belinda said. "The last time I trusted you, you got into the cookies and ended up with cookie whiskers. This time we could have stuck-together kitty. But I guess I have to give you a chance to be a good boy, so I'm going to begin."

"Let's see," Belinda said quietly as she reached under the bed. "I'll need glue pots and paper and scissors. AND scraps of old dresses and sequins and tiny sparklies."

With her tongue sticking out, Belinda concentrated on turning scraps and glue and sparklies into something special. She noticed that Custard looked over and peeked at her project from time to time.

"What do you think, Custard?" Belinda asked. "I'm making a picture for my parents with people AND a little house AND a car AND even a kitty!"

"AND I'm drawing a picture for Grandmother that looks just like me in a magical green dress!"

Well, as you might expect, Custard couldn't see very well from where he was. The moment Belinda's back was turned, he leaped onto the floor to check out the pictures. As he did, he spilled glue pots and sparklies all over himself. When Belinda heard the noise, she turned to see a gold and silver kitty, all sparkly and very, very angry. She picked up the glue pot before any glue could spill on her soft old rug. She then looked at her kitty, with his sparkly fur all fluffed out in a tantrum.

"Custard," she said, "now look what you've done. I gave you a chance to be a very good kitty and instead you've decorated yourself. First the cookies and now the sparklies." Then, her stern little girl voice changed to a giggle. "But you were just doing what I was doing, weren't you, Custard? I was making a special picture for Mommy and Daddy and Gramps AND one for Grandmother, and you made a special picture for me. But I wish that next time you would use paper for your drawings, instead of your very own self!"

And with great kitty cat disdain, Custard slunk away to the dark and slumberous place beneath Belinda's bed. There he could lick away the sparklies before anyone else witnessed his humiliation. Poor old Custard. He would never grow to be a great, proud grown-up cat at this rate!

Belinda, meanwhile, was putting the finishing touches on her pictures. She tucked them into the space behind her dresser to dry, safe from dust rags, until she was ready to work on them again. When they dried, she would add little drawings and words with her watercolors, making extra special pictures for her family for Christmas. "Next time," thought Belinda, "I'll leave Custard downstairs. I don't think he'd like himself very much in watercolors." Then she giggled at the thought and scooted downstairs. She was just in time to help set the table.

"I'd better catch up on my Advent Calendar!" she said to her father. "Maybe I'll draw a picture of a Little Drummer Boy—with sparkles," she giggled.

December 13: On the Train

I'm not sure what Belinda is going to be doing today. However, her father was doing something with suitcases while Belinda was sleeping. Suitcases usually mean a trip. Do you remember something about Belinda going on a trip? Do YOU ever need suitcases to go on a trip? Does someone help you pack? (I'll bet they remember undies and socks!) I wonder what YOU would need if you were going to NEW YORK?

"Wake up, Belinda," her father whispered. "We have to get up extra early so we can catch the train to Grandmother's house."

"I'm awake!" Belinda said, practically jumping out of her bed in a single leap. "Oh boy, oh boy, oh boy, I'm awake and ready to go to Grandmother's!"

Her father laughed out loud at Belinda's energy. "I packed our bags last night, so we'll just have a quick breakfast and we WILL be ready to go. You'll need to get dressed and say goodbye to Custard, then come down to the kitchen as soon as you can."

Belinda raced to the closet and grabbed the clothing she would wear to New York. She noticed that her father had already taken the beautiful green Nutcracker dress and packed it in her suitcase. She smiled and picked comfortable shoes and socks for walking, her Sunday-best coat, a fluffy sweater, and warm pants for outdoor time.

Moving quickly, she remembered that she had not yet said good morning to Howard. So, she decided that she could do two things at one time. Or (she giggled) maybe three!

Patting Custard she said, "Good morning, Howard! I'm hurrying to get ready to go see Grandmother but wanted to say hello before I have to go. I hope You have a GREAT day today and that You will be in New York with my dad and grandmother and me. And please keep an eye on my gramps and Custard while we're gone. I love You!!"

Before you could say "Custard is one crazy kitty," Belinda was dressed, downstairs, and in the car, ready to go.

At the Princeton Junction station, Gramps dropped off Belinda and her father. They waved goodbye as they pulled their roll-aboard bags onto the train.

Once she was settled in her seat, Belinda wanted to know how long the train ride would take.

"Well," her father said, "it's about seventy-five minutes to Penn Station. When we get off the train, it's another fifteen minutes by car to Grandmother's house."

Belinda added up the minutes, counting on her fingers. It seemed like a lot of time from her house to Grandmother.

Counting minutes didn't help, and her fidget spinner didn't help. Her father asked her if she'd like to look at some pictures of New York and get ready for her visit.

"Would I!" she said as her father handed her a small book. She opened the book and the first thing she saw was a GIGANTIC tree! Her father said, "That's a Rockefeller Center Christmas tree. The trees come from forests far away, and every year a big truck brings a new tree to New York. The truck travels overnight so that no one sees the tree until it gets to Rockefeller Center."

Belinda turned the page, her eyes like saucers. "Look! People are ice skating right below the Christmas tree. Are we going to see all this while we visit Grandmother?"

"I think you will have to ask Grandmother about that. And we are almost there!"

Now Belinda REALLY wanted the train to go faster.

She tried to be the first to spy the very tall buildings she'd heard about, like the Empire State Building. Then, at last, she noticed that some things looked a little bit familiar.

"Dad," she asked her father. "Have I been here before? To New York City and Grandmother's house?"

"Of course," her father said. "When you were four years old, your mother was a doctor at a big hospital in Philadelphia, and we traveled to New York to see your grandmother. But it's been a while, and I'm surprised that you remember."

"Ohhh!" Belinda said. "I'm not sure I remember what she looks like exactly, but probably like my grandmother!"

And just like that, she noticed that it was very dark outside. Were they in a tunnel? She looked at her father with surprise, but he just smiled and said, "We're almost there. The train has to go underneath all the big buildings and the streets to get to the station."

In the blink of an eye, they were whisking their bags off the train, onto the platform, and up a giant escalator. Staying very close together in the crowd, they made their way to an exit where taxis were waiting. Belinda and her father entered the back seat of a yellow taxicab. Soon they were deep in the traffic of New York City streets, on their way to Grandmother's house.

Sam gave the driver the address, and Belinda was so excited she was practically spinning around in her seat. So many cars, so many people, so much to see!

Sam smiled at his daughter's energy and excitement. The streets of New York were familiar to him, but he knew that it was all new and exciting to Belinda.

As they drove, Sam pointed out some of the sights along the way. However, he wanted to let Belinda's grandmother have the fun of telling her what they would be doing in the afternoon.

"Belinda," he said, "I don't know how much you remember about your mommy's mother. She is always very dressed up and wears beautiful jewelry and looks very pretty. Her glasses aren't round and brown like mine, and she is kind of fancy. People in New York sometimes get dressed up more than people on our farm. But it's okay—you and I look just great!!"

As soon as the taxi pulled up at the tall house where her mommy grew up, Belinda looked up and saw her grandmother standing in the doorway and smiling. "You can go, Belinda," her father said. As he got their bags from the taxi, Belinda raced up the steps to her grandmother.

"Ah, tourists!!" Grandmother said, after hugging Belinda and Sam and walking into the house. "Today we are going to be tourists in the greatest city on earth! We will go to Rockefeller Center and see the tree and do some ice skating! Then we'll walk on Fifth Avenue and look in the shop windows. And when we get tired, we'll have afternoon tea at The Plaza."

"Like Eloise? At Eloise's Plaza?"

Grandmother smiled and nodded, chuckling at the thought of the elegant and famous Plaza Hotel being "Eloise's Plaza!"

"With tea under our belt, we'll be ready to go to Macy's department store to see the REAL Santa. After that we'll come back here for a light dinner, some Advent Calendar time, and off to bed for all of us!"

"Oh my!" Belinda said quietly. "I don't even know what some of those things are. But I am ready to be a tourist and learn about the city where my mommy grew up. Maybe tonight I will draw a TRAIN on my Advent Calendar!"

Sam looked at Belinda's grandmother and just shook his head. "Thank you for planning such a wonderful day. I hope you are ready for a bundle of energy that just doesn't quit."

"A bit like her mother—she never was still a minute either," Grandmother smiled. "New York—get ready—here comes Belinda!"

Soon, Sam carried their bags to Grandmother's guest rooms. Belinda looked all around, wondering which room had been her mother's. She peeked in a pretty bathroom and washed her hands with good-smelling soap. She sniffed her hands and looked at herself in the mirror. She felt that she was already very grown up—after that big train trip—and ready for a day in New York!

"Belinda," her grandmother said, "are you ready to go? New York is waiting for you!"

Belinda took her grandmother's hand and grinned her happiest smile. "I am SO ready, Grandmother!"

Sam and Belinda and her grandmother stepped outside. On the street, a black car was waiting to take them to their first destination: the world-famous Rockefeller Center.

In the car, Sam reminded Belinda that she would have to hold his hand whenever they were out on the street. New York was a crowded city, and he wanted to be sure they stayed together.

"No problem," mumbled Belinda, with her eyes glued to the windows. She'd never seen so much traffic or heard so many horns honking.

"Looks like a gazillion people," she said softly.

Suddenly the car slowed, and she said, "WHOA! Head explosion! Daddy, do you see that tree? And those angels? Are we getting out here—I hope, I hope, I hope?! Can we go see?"

While Sam opened the door, Grandmother took Belinda's hand, enjoying the excitement in her granddaughter's eyes.

"That tree looks just like the one in the book! It's the biggest, bestest, thing I have ever seen," Belinda said, walking as quickly as she could. "And there are gold statues and angels and ICE SKATERS and flags everywhere."

Turning to her grandmother, she asked, "Grandmother, did you KNOW it was going to be like this? Did my mommy ever see all this?"

"Oh, yes, Belinda," her grandmother said. They moved closer to the ice rink and looked down at children and grownups wobbling their way around.

"Wow," Belinda breathed. "I don't know how you could ever leave this."

"Ah," said her grandmother. "But part of what makes it so special is that it's only like this at Christmas. People come from all over the world to see the lights and the beautiful tree, and they love it just as much as you, Belinda."

"Wow. Just wow." Belinda said.

Her father looked at her and saw that "Belinda look" in her eye. "Did you want to go ice skating, Belinda?" he asked. "We don't have a lot of time, but we have a little."

And so they did. Grandmother rented skates for Belinda and her dad, and off they went. They held hands and skated round and round and round, making Grandmother's smile bigger and bigger and bigger.

If they didn't get to Fifth Avenue or the Plaza until tomorrow—well, that would be just fine with Grandmother! This was a day that all of them would remember!

When Belinda finally went to bed that night, her eyes were very heavy as she tried to store up memories to share with Custard and her Advent Calendar. But she would remember!!

December 14: Belinda Goes to The Nutcracker

Have you ever gone on a trip that was just MAGICAL? Maybe you went to the beach or to a high mountain. Or maybe you took a boat ride on a pretty lake. If you close your eyes and remember your special places, does that help you imagine how EXCITED Belinda is to see one of the most famous cities in the world? Whew! New York is a BIG city with very tall buildings, and a park where there are playgrounds and horses and even carriages. Along the streets at Christmastime, there are trees everywhere!

Blinking her eyes in the morning, Belinda looked around and wondered where she was. No Custard. A different comforter. Different smells and sounds. Was she having a dream?

"NO!" she said to herself in a moment. "I'm at Grandmother's house in New York City. And YESTERDAY we saw the tree at Rockefeller Center AND we ice skated and TODAY we are going to see The Nutcracker."

"Howard," whispered Belinda, "I know that You know where I am even though I'm somewhere different today. Please keep an eye on Custard and Gramps for me. I know they will miss us, but I hid an extra treat for Custard under my pillow, so I hope he finds it."

"And Howard," Belinda continued, "I promise to be very good when we go to The Nutcracker. But if I need some help with the jumpy jitters and start fidgeting around, I hope You'll be there with me so that Grandmother will be glad she invited me to come. I know she misses my mom, and maybe I can give her some extra hugs while I'm here.

"And one more thing, Howard: I LOVE YOU AND HOPE YOU HAVE A GREAT DAY!"

With that, Belinda was out of bed and off to start her special day in New York.

Wearing her beautiful new dress, Belinda smiled with a special glow when they reached the theater. Looking around, she turned to her grandmother and said, "I wish I had crayons and paper with me, so I could draw everything before I forget!"

Her grandmother smiled and helped Belinda settle into her seat. "Still looking around, Grandmother," she whispered! "That's okay," her grandmother whispered back. "Pretty soon your eyes will be busy watching the stage!"

Before long, members of the orchestra started playing something, but Belinda didn't like the music very much.

"Grandmother," she whispered. "That music doesn't sound very nice, you know. Not like the Nutcracker music on TV."

"You're right, Belinda," her grandmother chuckled. "That's not the Nutcracker music. It's the getting-ready music that's called 'tuning.' Each orchestra member has to make sure his or her instrument is in tune with all of the others. Does that make any sense to you, Belinda?"

"I guess so, but it certainly is a racket!" the little girl said. She sneaked a last peek around at all the pretty dresses and touched the soft green skirt of her own Nutcracker dress.

Just then a hush came over the audience and a bright light shone on the orchestra. People began applauding as one person, dressed in black, walked out from behind the curtains. She took her place between the audience and the orchestra. When the applause quieted, the lady in black raised a little stick and the racket was over for good! The wonderful music of The Nutcracker began. Belinda was so excited that she reached for her grandmother's hand, just to hold herself in her seat.

As the lights dimmed, the giant curtain began to rise. The curtain disappeared ever so slowly into the ceiling and, at last, Belinda could see what a ballet really was.

Two children, not much older than Belinda, were on the stage, trying to peer through a door. Why, I could do that, thought Belinda. Perhaps I should be a ballerina someday and wear lipstick, just like that little girl.

The children on the stage were peeking at preparations for a family Christmas party. There was a tree and presents and guests arriving. Belinda was surprised at how easy it was to figure out what was going on, even though no one said any words. With the music and costumes and the way the dancers moved, Belinda knew every single minute what was happening.

"Grandmother," she whispered, "when do we see the evil Mouse king? Is it soon?"

"No, Belinda," whispered her grandmother. "You must be patient and let them tell the story."

Belinda sighed. It was so beautiful she thought she would burst from watching. And just then, a magical thing began to happen. Right before her very eyes, the Christmas tree on the stage began to grow. And grow. And grow. And snow fell right on the stage, even though Belinda knew that they were indoors. And from that moment on, she did not pull her grandmother's sleeve or whisper about the Mouse King. Belinda, like a million girls before her, was lost in the magic of The Nutcracker.

When intermission came, Belinda's eyes were still glued to the stage, looking for more. "Oh, Grandmother," she said, "surely it isn't over!"

"Of course not, Belinda. But the dancers—and even the watchers—need a little rest. That is what intermission is for. Let's go see if they have some juice, then we'll come right back and be ready for more."

In the lobby, Belinda looked like there was a secret that she was thinking about. Looking up at her grandmother, she giggled. "Even though I was watching the dancers very carefully, there was one time I got bored for just a minute or two. So I started imagining what would happen on that stage if Custard got loose up there."

Her grandmother laughed.

"You're right, Belinda. He'd be up in the Christmas tree. He'd open all the presents, and then he'd probably try to dance with the ballerinas. I think they should put him in the show for next year!"

As they finished their juice, the lights began blinking in the lobby. Belinda looked puzzled.

"Let's go, Belinda," said her grandmother. "The blinking lights mean that the show is about to begin, and we need to be in our seats and ready to watch. It is discourteous to the performers to be late."

"All right, Grandmother," said Belinda. "I like The Nutcracker so much that I am trying to remember EVERY single minute so I can tell Daddy and Gramps and Custard and draw pictures on my Advent Calendar too!"

Her grandmother took her hand as they walked back to their seats. "Well, I hope your memory can hold a little more, because the best part is yet to come!"

At last the ballet was over, and the dancers came out on the stage for lots of applause. Belinda clapped until her hands were sore. "Oh," she sighed when the curtain closed for the last time and all the lights came back on. "Do they do that every single day? Just the same?"

"Well," her grandmother said, "The Nutcracker is a very popular ballet, and it is performed many times at Christmas. Sometimes there are different dancers so that the ones who have the hardest parts get a chance to rest. But the dancers practice for many years to be able to dance at this special theater in New York. They have to be very, very good, and it takes a lot of work and a lot of years to dance so well."

"I think I want to learn how to dance!" Belinda said. "I would like to twirl and dance and jump up and down just like the Nutcracker dancers!"

"Well," her grandmother said. "Your mother took ballet lessons when she was a little girl. So let's talk to your father about lessons for you when we go to tea."

She looked at her grandmother with a puzzled face. "Is tea a place where we go? I thought it was a yucky hot drink with lemon for coughing!"

While waving to their black car, her grandmother laughed. "No, tea is indeed a hot drink, but this one won't be yucky. We're going to meet your father at The Plaza, where we will have tea and small sandwiches and some yummy desserts. I think you will like it as much as Eloise did. And I'll bet watching The Nutcracker made you very hungry!"

"OFF to the Plaza!" said Belinda, her face peering out the window of the car. "Grandmother, I see horses and carriages. The horses have flowers, and they are taking people for rides. Is New York ALWAYS like this?"

Her grandmother smiled as they arrived at The Plaza. Belinda's father joined them, hugging his daughter as she exploded out of the car. "I LOVE NEW YORK," she said in her biggest outdoor voice. And everyone around them smiled because they loved New York too!

December 15: Soup and Santa

Have you been keeping track of Belinda's Advent Calendar? Let's see: We have a train and The Nutcracker and The Plaza and a smiling snowman and a happy heart with a cat inside, a Christmas tree farm. Hmmm. With a few more days left before Christmas, I wonder what Belinda will think of next? If YOU were going to draw a picture of What It Is That Makes It Christmas, what would you draw? I wonder if you could help Belinda figure it out!

Belinda whirled and twirled and spun, dancing to the music and bowing to the audience. People clapped and cheered and threw roses on the stage, and Custard had a front row seat. Stirring in her sleep, Belinda smiled a happy smile due to her magical and happy dreams.

Suddenly, a noise outside her door brought her fully back to her own world.

"Oh, Howard," said Belinda. "What a wonderful dream I had! I danced with the prince and wore beautiful costumes and it was just excellent." She sighed a contented sigh, then added, "And Custard was there too, sitting right up front in a velvet seat, all dressed up in a Christmas bow." She giggled as she tried to imagine Custard sitting still long enough to put a bow around his neck!

"Well, Howard," she said, "I guess my dream wasn't very real, but I wanted to thank You for a SUPER PERFECT DAY yesterday. And today Dad and I are going to stay at Grandmother's house for a while. Dad said we are going to be 'giving back.' I don't know what we're giving back, but I sure hope it isn't Custard or The Nutcracker or my special dress!"

Grinning, she jumped out of bed. She wished Howard a SUPER PERFECT DAY TOO and ran out to the kitchen in tiny dancer steps. Then she stopped dead in her tracks. On the counter in the kitchen was a mountain! There were piles of cans and boxes and baskets in all sizes, colors, and shapes. So many that Belinda could just barely see her grandmother by peeking around the mountain.

"Oh my goodness," she said to her father and Grandmother. "What is all this stuff? And why is it all over the kitchen? Are we going to be a supermarket?"

"Good morning, Belinda," her grandmother chuckled. "I see that you still like to ask at least three questions at a time, but I will do my best to answer them. No, we are not going to be a supermarket. It's all over our kitchen because we have to get it packed up. AND this stuff is exactly what it looks like!"

“Oh, Grandmother,” said Belinda. “You know that what I really want to know is what’s going on. And if it’s something I can help with.”

“Indeed you can, Belinda,” said her father as he reached around the mountain to pull her into a hug. “Your grandmother is just teasing you, but I will tell you just what this is all about.”

“Every week of the year, our family—here in New York and at Gramps’s house—always buys some extra things at the store. Sometimes we buy four cans of soup or four cans of stew or four cans of vegetables or four cans of fruit or gravy or whatever. Grandmother taught your mommy to do that from the time she was very small. And your Gramps and I do the same thing at our house. In fact, lots of our friends do it too, though some people can only buy three cans a week or two or one.”

“This year, as you can see, Grandmother has accumulated a lot of food for the poor people.”

“Wow!” said Belinda. “Now I understand.” And she paused for a moment. “But why are you gathering them up this morning?”

As her father began to speak, Belinda interrupted him with great excitement. “Wait, wait, wait,” she said. “I bet I can guess! The cans are for people who don’t have enough money to buy food for their families at Christmastime. And people that do have enough buy extra—is that it, is that it, is that it?”

Belinda’s father and grandmother beamed with pride. “That’s exactly it!” her grandmother said. “And how clever you are to figure it out all on your own. We deliver food to the local Food Bank throughout the year, but we try extra hard at Christmastime.”

“Grandmother,” said Belinda, “I have some money saved up and I would like to buy the poor people some soup too!”

“Belinda,” her grandmother said, “your mother would be so proud to hear that. It is always a good idea to think of your money as having three parts. Some for saving, some for spending, and some for helping. In our family, lots of people remember the part about helping, and you will see how you can help too.”

“What can I do, what can I do, what can I do?” asked Belinda.

“Well, Belinda,” said her father. “First we are going to have breakfast so that all of us have lots of energy. After that, you can help Grandmother and me to pack the food into baskets and boxes.”

“After that,” her dad continued, “your grandmother will make arrangements to have the food delivered to a local Food Bank, where people can come and pick it up. This afternoon, you and I will take the train back home. And you will already be an experienced packer, so you can help Gramps and me with the food and supplies that we have ready at our house. Gramps likes to mix it up a bit, so we'll have baskets of flour and sugar and oatmeal too. Then other girls can make cookies for Christmas, just like we did.”

“Daddy,” said Belinda, “when we make our baskets at home, could we put some of our homemade cookies in the basket too? I would like to give something that I made with my very own hands.”

Belinda's father and grandmother smiled at each other. They were pleased that Belinda wanted to be a part of the “giving back.”

And just as Belinda reached out for a “whole family hug,” her elbow bumped a can, which bumped another can, which bumped another can.

Only a few cans landed on the floor, but Belinda could not stop giggling. "I know," said Belinda, "that Custard is not here, but even when he's far away, it seems like crazy things can happen. When we make the baskets at home, we'd better make sure Custard is NOT in the kitchen!"

All of them had a good laugh at the thought of Custard teetering at the top of a canned goods mountain, with soup flying and baskets rolling across the floor.

Belinda giggled again. "At least we'll be ready for him," she said. She picked up cans and placed them back on the counter. "I think I may have to draw some soup cans on my Advent Calendar today!"

"But there's one more thing to do before we go home, Belinda," her father said, with a twinkle in his eye. "Remember when we first came to Grandmother's house? She said we would see Rockefeller Center, and the ice skating, and the windows on Fifth Avenue—which we will have to see next time. And there was one more thing. I wonder if you remember?"

While looking from her father to her grandmother, Belinda's eyes got bigger and bigger. "You mean the REAL Santa at Macy's?"

"That's what I mean," her father said. "We will go to Macy's and see Santa before we go home. How does that sound?"

"HOT, HOT, HOT," called Belinda over her shoulder as she ran to her room to get her favorite Christmas sweater.

In just a few seconds, she was back. She pulled her sweater over her head and pulled shoes over her sockless feet. Her father laughed and helped her find her socks and warm clothing to wear.

Going to Macy's meant another black car ride, because Grandmother didn't like walking all the steps to use the subway, so off they went again. In the car, Belinda's father said, "You know, Belinda, sometimes there is a long line to see Santa, so we might have to wait a bit. But I made sure we would have plenty of time before our train, so just be patient and it will be fine."

"Do you know what you want for Christmas?" Grandmother asked.

Belinda was very quiet. "I think," she said, "that what I want can't come down a chimney. I want my mommy to come home and I want a whole family hug."

"I understand," her father said. "And you are right that the best presents of all can't come down a chimney. But think about something you might like to do or give or share or play with—something that can come down a chimney. And it's okay to tell Santa about the part he can't do. He'll understand too."

The line was long, but it was worth it. And Grandmother took a wonderful picture of Belinda sitting on Santa's lap and asking for a present that can't come down a chimney. Grandmother knew that Belinda's mother would love that picture very, very much.

December 16: Show and Tell

Hmmm. Belinda's mother called it "giving back." Like giving something to others when you already have what you need. Belinda and her family have plenty of food, but "giving" reminded her of the Nativity scene at her house. The Wise Men brought presents to the Baby Jesus. They probably had lots left over and could give presents. But even simple people could give little gifts. I wish I could put a can of soup next to Belinda's nativity scene, so she'd get the idea! But let's see what happens next—she's trying hard to answer her mother's question!

Belinda woke up in her own bed after the exciting weekend in New York. She danced her fingers across the pillow and around the bed, capturing her kitty and pulling him close.

"Good morning, Custard. And Good morning Howard! I had a SUPER PERFECT TIME in New York with Grandmother, but I'm glad to be back home with Custard and Gramps again. I know I have to go to school today, but I wanted to ask You… Can You hurry and bring my mommy home for Christmas? I haven't said anything to my dad or to Gramps because I know they miss her a lot too. But Grandmother seemed to be missing her also, and that's an awful lot of missing. So if You could hurry her up, I would be VERY happy! And I hope You have a SUPER DAY today. I love You!"

Jumping out of bed, Belinda peeked in her closet to see if her favorite jeans and bright red sweater were ready to wear. "Christmas sweater," she mumbled to herself. "I would like to wear my nice red Christmas sweater today! And there it is!"

Pulling on her clothing and socks and slippers, she headed for the kitchen, ready for breakfast and another December day. She wouldn't tell anyone about praying for her mommy to come home—she didn't want to make them sad. She'd just keep it a secret between her and Howard.

"Isn't it getting close to bedtime?" Gramps asked, glancing at the clock.

"I just got up, Gramps! Are you teasing me?"

Chuckling, Gramps said, "I was just making sure you were paying attention, Belinda. All that travel to New York could make anybody a little tired. Even Custard!"

"Custard's never tired, Gramps," Belinda laughed. "He probably sleeps all day when we're not around, except when he's getting into trouble."

“Good morning, Belinda,” her father said. “I see you’re wearing your favorite Christmas sweater. Is today a special day at school?”

“YES!” Belinda said. “It is Show and Tell today, and I know exactly what I want to bring.”

“I can’t wait to hear,” her father said. “As long as it isn’t Custard!”

“Well,” Belinda giggled, “not exactly.”

Raising his eyebrows, Belinda’s father wondered what “Not exactly” might mean.

“Well,” said Belinda, “it is Show and Tell, so I want to SHOW them my favorite poem. I also want to TELL them why my name is Belinda and why my kitty’s name is Custard.”

“That is a GREAT idea,” said Belinda’s father as he put a bowl of cereal and berries on Belinda’s placemat. “And I know you will do a great job telling the story!”

Belinda smiled. She was pleased that her father agreed that “The Tale of Custard the Dragon” was a perfect story for Show and Tell. Belinda finished her breakfast and got her coat and boots. Meanwhile, her father went upstairs and fetched the book that held the much-loved poem.

“Do you think you will read them the whole poem?” her father asked, “or will you just tell them the important parts?”

“I think I will SHOW them the poem and TELL them the story,” Belinda said. “I have thought about this a lot, and sometimes people ask me about my name. NOW they will know. And the part about Custard being a hero will be a great part of the story!”

Later, Belinda sat on the floor with the class. Her teacher announced that for today's Show and Tell, Belinda would be showing them a favorite poem and telling them an important story.

"A long time ago," Belinda began, "my parents decided that if they had a little girl, they wanted her to be very, very brave. They knew that sometimes hard things happen, and sometimes things aren't perfect. They wanted to be sure that any little girl they had would be able to handle lots and lots of things."

Holding up the book, she read the title: "The Tale of Custard the Dragon" by Ogden Nash.

As she opened the book, she looked around at her friends and read her favorite part in her most dramatic voice: "Belinda was as brave as a barrel full of bears."

"Well," she continued, "when my mom and dad read that line in that poem, they decided that they wanted THEIR little girl to be as brave as a barrel full of bears. They promised that, if they had a little girl one day, they would name her Belinda."

Looking around at her friends and smiling proudly, she said, "And so, of course, that's why my name is Belinda."

Looking at the book again, she said, "My parents started reading this poem to me when I was very little. I decided then that if I ever had a kitty, I would name him Custard. He could be just like Custard the Dragon in the poem—really squishy and kind of scared on the outside but brave on the inside when it matters.

"I know we don't have time today, but I am writing a story about something that happened last week when my cat, Custard, was a hero. So next time, for Show and Tell, I'll tell you the story of Custard the Hero. And my dad printed copies of this poem, so I could give you a copy for yourselves. And that's my Show and Tell. Thank you!"

Belinda's friends were very excited that she had her own poem. They all took their copies home, promising to ask their families about where THEIR names came from. Belinda thought they were probably hoping that their names were as brave as a barrel full of bears too. But she wasn't counting on it!

She wondered if she could draw a barrel full of bears on her Advent Calendar, then giggled at such a funny idea!

December 17: Invitations

Wow! From The Nutcracker to The Plaza to Show and Tell! Belinda is very busy—and today is the 17th! Christmas is only EIGHT days away. I wonder if Belinda talked to any of her friends about the Advent Calendar and her ideas for What It Is That Makes It Christmas? Maybe she will talk to them today! Let's find out!

"Shhh, Custard," Belinda said. "I hear you thinking!"

Then she giggled at the idea of Custard being able to think out loud. Belinda scratched her itchy nose.

"Howard," she said, "good morning! That silly cat must have walked on my head again because my nose is itchy. But it's time to get up anyway. And I wanted to remember to say thank You for such a GREAT Show and Tell yesterday. I know that I DID the Show and Tell, but I think that You helped me out a lot with good ideas. And telling my friends about how I got my name was a really special one."

Rolling over and scratching Custard behind the ear, she continued, "I don't know what we're doing today, but it seems like EVERY day is a great day. Well, mostly great. I haven't talked to you about my mommy lately and I miss her an awful lot. But my dad and grandmother say she will probably be coming home pretty soon. So maybe You could just keep an extra careful eye on her till she gets here!"

With that, she was off and running, bounding into her day as she so often did. She was ready for anything that came her way.

"Hello, Belinda!" her father said as Belinda raced into the kitchen. "I can see that you're wide awake and ready for your next-to-last day of school before Christmas vacation!"

"Oh boy," Belinda said. "And it's a half day, right? Does that mean we'll do something special this afternoon, like bake cookies or wrap presents or make some more food baskets?"

"Let's see," her father said. "I thought maybe you'd stopped thinking in threes, but I guess not! And actually we're going to do something different this afternoon that we haven't done yet. You and I are going to plan a party AND make invitations AND send them out. So I guess that comes in threes after all!"

"A party! What kind of party? At our house? Can I invite my friends?"

"A Christmas party, yes and yes, Belinda. We are going to decorate the barn and invite people to come over and share cookies and do some Christmas crafts and read some stories. You remember that Gramps used to use the barn when he was a vet and took care of people's animals? Well, he had it cleaned up recently and it is all ready for a party."

"Oh boy!" Belinda cried. "If it's a Christmas party, it has to be very soon—Christmas Eve is only a week away! Where do we start?"

Smiling at Belinda's usual enthusiasm, her father said, "When you get home from school, we'll start by making a list of people we'd like to invite. It's not a lot of notice—just a few days—but the party will be an Open House. That means people can come and go when it's convenient for them, because everyone has a lot to do at the holidays."

The minute Belinda got home from school, she grabbed a tablet and pencil and began writing the names of her friends. Before long, she and her father had a list of children and parents and friends and were ready to begin making invitations.

"If we only needed one or two, I'd make them by hand," Sam said. "But I think we have enough names on our list to make our invitations on the computer."

Sam and Belinda sat side by side at the desk in the big kitchen. On the computer, they searched for an easy way to design and print their own invitations. In less than fifteen minutes, they had chosen a design that was just right—a picture of a barn all decorated for Christmas!

Belinda helped write the words while her dad worked on the picture.

"Okay," Belinda said. "Here are some good words."

Jingle bells, jingle bells, jingle all the way

Come and have some fun with us

At our barn on Saturday!!!

"Perfect," Belinda's father said. "Now we also want to tell them the address, the time, and what we will be doing. Sometimes it's nice to let people know that they don't have to get dressed up, so we'll do that too!"

Christmas cookie sharing

Story reading

Christmas crafts

And lots of good things to eat!

Belinda's Barn

1 pm to 5 pm

Saturday, December 21

Be ready to sit on the floor—jeans are okay!!

"Huh," said Belinda. "Are we all done now? Do we print them out? Can we deliver them to people?"

"Yes, we're done, and we can print them. I think delivering them by hand is a great idea since there are not very many days left if we put them in the mail. So let's get started!"

With the printer pumping out invitations, Belinda grabbed envelopes and the list. She made sure that everyone on the list had an envelope, ready for the invitation.

"This is going to be one GREAT party," said Belinda. Looking up at her father, she decided she was probably not going to like the answer to her next question. But she asked it anyway.

"Dad," Belinda said sweetly, "can Custard come to the party?"

Without even waiting for an answer, she shook her head sadly. She knew the risks. What if he got out and ran away again? Oh no. Custard would just have to hear about the party from Belinda. That would just have to do.

Belinda quietly tucked one of the invitations in her pocket because it showed a picture of a barn. She would draw a picture of a barn for her Advent Calendar, just like the barn for the party!

December 18: Christmas Caroling

Have you been keeping track? Did you notice that it's the last day of school before Christmas vacation? Do you do special things at your school when it's the last day before Christmas vacation? Do you have candy canes or cookies? Do you like to bring a present to your teacher? Let's see what Belinda is up to today!

"What a busy day," Belinda said to her father at Wednesday night supper. "I didn't even have time to talk to Howard this morning. I had to get ready to go right from home to school to supper to the Jolly Trolley!"

Smiling, her father helped Belinda fill her plate. He made sure she took something besides spaghetti, meatballs, and cake.

"I don't think Howard will mind," her father said. "I am sure you will find time to talk to Him before you go to sleep tonight. And besides, I'll bet that He is very happy that you are going Christmas caroling on the Jolly Trolley."

Belinda looked at the salad her father was piling on the side of her plate. She sighed and agreed that Howard might well like caroling more than she liked salad.

Once seated at their table, Belinda waited till she had time to munch some spaghetti before asking her father a question. It was a question she had never thought about before.

"Dad," she said, careful to swallow first, "how can we tell what it is that makes Howard happy? Sometimes I tell Him to have a really great day, but I'm not sure what a great day would be for Him! It's probably not about playing with a kitty or making cookies or drawing pictures. But I HOPE He has great days for sure!"

Her father looked very serious for a moment. "That, Belinda, is an excellent question. And I don't know that anyone knows the whole answer. But I know someone who might know part of it anyway."

Glancing across the room, Sam spotted Pastor John and walked over to see him. They spoke for a moment, and the two of them came back to the table and sat down with Belinda.

Pastor John was VERY tall, and as she looked up at him, Belinda was a little worried that maybe this was an answer she should already have known. But she noticed that her father and Pastor John were smiling. In fact, Pastor John reached out and shook Belinda's hand, without even checking for meatball stains.

“Belinda,” Pastor John said, “I hope you don’t mind that your dad shared your question with me. I liked it so much that I’d like to share it with all the people here at Wednesday night supper. I suspect that we will get lots and lots of answers, but I won’t do it if it’s not okay with you.”

“Oh!” said Belinda. “Will we still have time to go on the Jolly Trolley?”

“Of course,” Pastor John laughed. I’m planning to do some singing myself and wouldn’t miss it for the world. Just give me a quick minute to talk to people while they are still enjoying their dinners.”

And with that, Pastor John walked to the back of the room and picked up a microphone. As he always did at Wednesday night supper, he said a brief blessing. And he said a special thanks to Maria and Maria in the kitchen who made all the good food! But then he surprised everyone and told them about Belinda’s question. He said that he liked the question so much he wanted to know if people had some ideas about what would be a great day for God!

Answers came from all over the room! Mr. Witherby called out from his wheelchair, “Thankfulness makes God happy.”

And Miss Mary, the Sunday School teacher, said, “Kindness makes God happy.”

Wally the Sexton said, “Doing your best makes God happy.”

Belinda’s teacher said, “Doing your homework makes God happy!” Parents laughed at that one!

"Laughter makes God happy," said a new mother.

"Having supper together makes God happy," called a voice from the big church kitchen. That one got applause from all the people who loved Miss Maria's cooking. Especially from the kids who'd enjoyed their spaghetti and meatballs.

"Second chances make God happy," said a grandmother who smiled at all the children. "Even when there's a lot of talk about naughty and nice lists, God is very big on giving second chances."

Answers kept flying around the room from old people and children and parents and teachers.

Belinda raised her hand and said, "Christmas vacation makes KIDS happy!"

Whew! Pastor John wished he had known there would be so many—he would have written them down.

Finally, they heard the ding, ding of the Jolly Trolley. They knew it was time to climb aboard and ride around their community, checking out the Christmas lights and singing Christmas carols wherever they went.

Pastor John stood at the front of the Jolly Trolley just before they pulled away. He said, "I am thinking of one more thing that makes God happy!"

"What, what, what?" Belinda asked. "What could we possibly have missed?"

"SINGING," said Pastor John. He burst into a joyful "Jingle Bells," starting their ride on the Jolly Trolley with laughter, energy, kindness, enthusiasm—and a nice, big voice!

Singing along, Belinda wondered if she could draw a Jolly Trolley and some happy people. Just thinking about it made her smile!

December 19: A Special Sleepover

Have you been keeping track? Did you notice that yesterday was the last day of school before Christmas vacation? Are you surprised that Belinda didn't draw a picture of Santa or the reindeer or hanging Christmas stockings? Do YOU think maybe that's what Christmas is all about? Not many days left—we'd better see what she's doing today!

Belinda was the first one into the car after the Jolly Trolley ride. She managed to fasten her seat belt and pat her tummy at the same time. "Yum. I love it when we have spaghetti at Wednesday night supper! AND it made me think about having a sleepover with Elizabeth tomorrow night!"

"Spaghetti made you think about having a sleepover?" her father asked, as he buckled himself into his seat.

"NO," said Belinda, "but I got to see Elizabeth and have fun at dinner. THAT made me think that I haven't had Elizabeth come over for a sleepover in a VERY long time. AND there's no school tomorrow so she could come EARLY AND we wouldn't be any trouble AND we could play Twister and watch Christmas movies and eat popcorn and..."

"Sounds great!" her father said. "I'm sold. I will call Elizabeth's mom when we get home."

"Hurray! I will tell Custard when I get home. I'll start thinking about games we can play and movies we can watch. Awesome!"

By dinnertime on Thursday, Belinda had lined up at least eleven nail polish bottles on her dresser (just in case they needed manicures!). She also pulled out her favorite Christmas movies, like Frozen and Rudolph and Frosty and...

Waiting at the door, she heard the crunch of tires as Elizabeth's mom pulled into the driveway. "They're here, they're here, they're here!"

Running out in the cold without a coat, Belinda wrapped her arms around her friend Elizabeth for a huge hug. "Can you believe it was only last week that we couldn't find you and we couldn't find Custard? And now here you are for a sleepover!"

The two girls grinned and raced into the warm kitchen, arm in arm.

Sam greeted Elizabeth's mother. He asked if she would like to come in for coffee or a cup of tea, but she had to be on her way. Christmas errands, she said. Lots to do! She hugged her daughter and wished both girls a fun sleepover—with plenty of sleep!!

They giggled and looked at each other, wiggling their eyebrows. They knew that sleep was not at the top of their list of fun things to do.

"Come on, Elizabeth," Belinda said, tugging her friend to the closet. "We have to hang up your coat and put away your boots and wash our hands. I'm hoping for mac and cheese tonight, but I don't know for sure."

"I love mac and cheese!" Elizabeth beamed as she kicked her boots off. She was a lot like Belinda—she had only one speed and that was FAST!

Soon, Gramps and Belinda's dad and Elizabeth and Belinda were seated around the table. As always, Gramps said Grace. Belinda's nose looked like a bunny's as she sniffed around the covered dish on the table. Her father had to laugh at the bunny sniffing, and he put her out of her misery. He whisked the cover off a fragrant bowl of mac and cheese. The best kind, too! Crusty on top, just the way Belinda liked it.

Gramps and Sam pretended not to notice the little girls kicking each other under the table. It was a kind of secret code that meant, "Hurry up and eat so we can go play!"

Soon enough they were excused. They did not even have to help clear the table—a special treat for sleepover night!

Making their way to Belinda's room, the girls carried Elizabeth's small case upstairs. They put away her PJs and toothbrush and other stuff and greeted Custard with great respect!

Elizabeth noticed the nail polish bottles lined up in a row and raised her eyebrows. Were they going to give each other a manicure?

Belinda nodded. "Do you want to? We'd have to put a towel on the floor, so we don't make a mess, but it could be fun! AND there's a game called Spin the Bottle where you spin the bottles around to choose what color you want."

"I think I'd rather pick my own color, though. How about you?"

Elizabeth agreed. "Yellow and blue are my favorites," she said as she reached for a bottle of DARK BLUE polish. "WOW!" said Belinda. "I love that." Belinda chose dark green, the color of her new green dress.

After careful painting, finger wiping, and leaving only the tiniest bit on their faces, they were ready to go downstairs and show off their new nails.

"WHOA!" said Gramps. "Amazing! I thought nail polish only came in pink and red."

"Oh no, Gramps," said Belinda. "It comes in LOTS of colors."

Her father admired their hands. He asked if they might like to make a movie to send to Belinda's mother—they could sing a Christmas carol or just wave their hands a lot. She would love it no matter what they did, and he could make the movie with his phone!

"Ooooh, a movie," said Elizabeth.

"I know," Belinda said. "We could sing 'Jingle Bells.' We are very good at that one!"

And so they sang and waved their hands with blue and green nails flying above their heads with joy. With movies and popcorn and Twister ahead, it was sure to be a happy, happy night for everyone.

December 20: Fire Trucks and Dalmatians

Wow—the morning after a sleepover. Now THAT is special!

Belinda cocked one eye at the calendar on the wall. She was not sure if she wanted to wake all the way up yet or not. But as she shifted in her comfy bed, she noticed that there was something larger than Custard beside her! Elizabeth! And she was still asleep!

"Howard," she whispered, "I am going to say a very FAST good morning because I have a lot to do today. But I want to thank You for the sleepover with my friend Elizabeth, and I hope You have a great day. And maybe You could help make sure that I do a super, duper job tonight on the FIRE TRUCK! Love YOU."

Belinda's feet hit the ground so quickly that she was halfway out the door before Custard even woke up!

As she approached the kitchen, she heard her father say, "How's the weather looking, Dad?" Belinda guessed why her father was asking. This was the day when the fire trucks would deliver toys and food, and her father was probably hoping it wouldn't be a rainy or snowy night.

Racing into the kitchen, Belinda said, "I don't care if it rains and snows elephants! I will ride a fire truck tonight and help Santa deliver toys and food."

"Good morning, Belinda," her father said. "I guess you are just a little bit excited about riding the fire truck!"

Taking her seat at the table, Belinda said, "I am VERY excited, but my friend Elizabeth wants to know how come I get to ride the fire truck."

"Yes indeed I do!" Elizabeth said, wrapping her robe around her and joining Belinda at the table. "I really would like to know." While the girls hugged each other, Sam said to Belinda, "It's because of your grandfather. Every year the town honors someone who has made a difference by inviting a member of their family to ride the truck. This year our family was chosen to honor Gramps for the time when he was a veterinarian and took care of a special Dalmatian that rode on a fire truck."

"I know about Dalmatians!" Belinda said. "They are big white dogs with black spots—or big black dogs with white spots!!"

"I know about Dalmatians too," said Elizabeth. "They can run very fast!"

"Both of you are right," Gramps chuckled. "A long time ago, a brave Dalmatian named Quincy saved people from a burning house. And ever since then, every firehouse in our town has a Dalmatian named Quincy."

"Gramps saved that first Quincy from burns he suffered in the fire," Sam said. "And the town never forgot. SO this year, you, Belinda, get to ride the fire truck as a way for the town to say thank you to Gramps for his special gift of healing a firehouse dog."

"WOW!" Belinda said. "I never heard that story before. "Will I get to meet a Quincy at the firehouse?"

"You bet," Gramps said.

Elizabeth was sad that she had to go home after breakfast. That night, she would be sure to be watching for the fire truck and waving to her friend Belinda!

Belinda and Sam and Gramps drove to the firehouse right after lunch, so they could help pack up the toys and food that the trucks would be delivering. Sunset would be around 4:30 that day, and that's when deliveries would begin. It seemed a lot more magical for the fire trucks to come in the dark since Santa would be on board!

Belinda learned that each fire truck had closets that usually held hoses and other firefighter stuff. But today, they were filling the closets with bags of toys and food. Each bag had to match a list of addresses, to be sure everything ended up in the right place.

"I know!" Belinda said. "If you take things to the wrong place, grandmothers could end up with skateboards and babies might get bicycles!"

One of the firefighters laughed. He agreed that getting gifts to the right people was an important job. Soon, Belinda was busy helping to check the list.

By 4:15, all of the closets on the fire trucks were filled, and the lists checked. Everyone was watching the clock, waiting for 4:30.

While they waited, Belinda had a question—or, actually, three questions—for one of the firefighters.

"What would happen if there was a real fire tonight, while we are out in the fire truck with Santa? Would we ride to the fire with you? Would Santa and I have to walk home?"

The firefighter smiled. "That's a good question, Belinda, but another firehouse is on call tonight. If there were a HUGE fire and our truck had to go too, we would send you and Santa home in the fire chief's car. It's our job to make sure we are prepared to fight a fire even when we have special passengers—and a truck full of toys! We think that keeping people safe is a special gift that we are able to give all year round. And it's extra special at Christmastime!"

"Hmmm," said Belinda. "I guess that's a relief, but it might be exciting to ride to a fire with you. It would be even better if I could bring my cat, Custard, along!"

“I think I heard about Custard,” the firefighter said. “Is that the kitty that helped save a little girl from getting run over by a car?”

“YES!” Belinda shouted. “That’s my cat!”

The firefighter smiled and said, “Why don’t you and Custard come and visit us one day? Firefighters like heroes a lot—even when they have four legs!!”

Soon, a loud bell rang. It was time for Belinda to climb up on the fire truck next to Santa and Quincy the Dalmatian.

“WOW!” Belinda said to Santa. “I think this might be the awesomest thing I have ever done. And NOW I get to help you give out presents!”

Just like Santa, she held on carefully, smiled her best smile, and waved at the people all along the street. What a great Christmas this was turning out to be, and Christmas Day was still four days away. She wasn’t sure how much more Christmas she could hold, but she knew what she would draw on her Advent Calendar tonight—a big red fire truck and maybe a big Dalmatian too. What a lot of stories she would tell Custard when she got home!

December 21: A Party at Belinda's Barn

FOUR more days! Belinda is excited about all the great things she's been doing this year, and she is faithfully drawing on her Advent Calendar every single day. But she's thinking harder and harder about What It Is That Makes It Christmas. If it's not the tree or the snow or the reindeer or Santa or stockings—then, what can it be? Maybe today's party will give her some more ideas! Let's see…

"Good morning, Howard," Belinda said softly from her cozy bed. "I think I just heard Gramps pulling out of the driveway in his truck. It's awful early for him to be going somewhere on a Saturday morning. I hope everything is okay!"

Giggling, she tickled Custard and continued. "Maybe he decided that we needed BACON and DOUGHNUTS for breakfast. Prob'ly not, but you never know!"

Custard rolled onto his back. He was hoping for belly scratches before Belinda jumped into her day and left him behind. She smiled, scratched, and said a quick THANK YOU to Howard before bouncing off her bed and into another amazing day!

No one was in the kitchen, but there was a note on the table from Belinda's father. It said, "I'm in the barn, decorating. Get your warm clothing and come join me!"

In her hurry, Belinda nearly tripped over Custard. She pulled a parka and boots over her Wonder Woman PJs and ran outside to the barn. She was plenty warm enough and didn't want to miss a minute.

When she pushed open the big old barn door, she gasped at the sight of tiny white fairy lights all around the barn. And her father gasped at the sight of Belinda's outfit, which was unusual to say the least!

"This is SO beautiful," Belinda said. "Can I help? What a great party we are going to have today!"

Sam smiled. "You absolutely can help! Gramps already put tables in the stalls where animals used to be so that we could set up some Christmas crafts. You can help me carry supplies to the stalls. I think we'll have crayons and paper and glue in one stall, in case anyone else wants to make an Advent Calendar. Then I'd like to have construction paper and glue in another stall."

"Oh!" Belinda said. "That's for paper chains! I love making paper chains!"

Sam showed his daughter the bags of craft supplies, sitting on a table.

"Belinda, why don't you decide which stall we'll use for which activity? Then you can take the right supplies to the right stall."

"I can do that in one quick minute," Belinda said, hurrying to get started on such a fun project.

When the barn door opened, Belinda saw a neighbor arrive with more tables. "Hi, Jeff!" Sam called. "Can you put the tables up here near the door? We'll want everyone to be able to find food and drink when they get hungry! Thank you for lending us your extra tables—we can use them today!"

Belinda was busy setting out construction paper and glue and scissors (grown-up scissors and play scissors). But she took a minute to peek around the corner of the stall. The old barn was starting to look like a place where a party was going to happen very soon!

In a few short minutes, Belinda had another stall ready, this time with paper and crayons and even a few markers. Kids might want to do Advent Calendars or just cards for their parents or pictures for their trees!

When the barn door opened again, it was Gramps. And he was carrying a BIG, BIG Christmas tree! Belinda gasped as she watched Gramps and her dad set the tree in a stand in a corner of the barn. Strings of lights came in next and were plugged in for testing. "Fairyland," whispered Belinda!

“Oh, Gramps,” she said. “That’s a great tree, but it doesn’t look like Clarence. Did you get TWO trees?”

“You bet,” said Gramps. “Clarence is resting in a bucket of cold water in the garage. He is getting used to the warmer temperature before we take him into the house later today.”

Belinda helped her father put the lights on the tree in the barn. As she did, she had a lot of questions—or at least three…

“How will we get this tree decorated in time? And did we make enough cookies for all the people who are coming? And why is the big rocker sitting in the corner near the tree? And…”

When she paused for breath, her father tackled the questions one at a time. “We’ll get the tree decorated in time by inviting everyone who comes to the party to put ornaments on it. AND we have groceries from the store to add to our supply of cookies. AND the big rocker is there so we can have kind of a Christmas story hour.

“I’m thinking we’ll put out some books—like How the Grinch Stole Christmas and The Night Before Christmas. And parents can sit in the rocker and read stories. Any kid who wants to hear a story can sit on the floor and listen. Sometimes kids get bored if they have to do the same thing for too long. So they might want to go from paper chains to drawing pictures, trimming the tree, eating cookies, and even story time.”

“WOW!” Belinda said. “I can’t wait till my friends come! This is going to be a GREAT, GREAT, GREAT party!”

“I hope so,” Sam said. “After you and Gramps and I have breakfast, we’ll get dressed for the party. We’ll bring cookies and juice and snowflake napkins and plates and lots of ornaments out here for our guests. I'm counting on lots of help from you, Belinda. I'm especially counting on you to keep Custard out of the barn today."

Belinda giggled. "Custard already has some experience with glue and sparklies! I think he's probably happy to stay in the house and have a good nap while we have a SUPER AWESOME GOOD party in the barn!"

On the way back to the house, Belinda asked her father about helping kids to draw Advent Calendars, and even giving them some ideas.

"I think that would be wonderful, Belinda! And I'll bet you'll get some new ideas for the last few days of YOUR calendar as well!"

"Maybe even a picture of a party," said Belinda as she skipped back to the house in her red rubber boots.

December 22: Christmas Pageant

Wow! I'll bet you wish you could have gone to Belinda's party too! Do you like to make paper chains or draw pictures—or eat cookies? If you're like Belinda, you still have a lot of energy, and you'll need it for today's adventure. Let's see what's happening!

Belinda must have turned over in her sleep once too often, because Custard jumped off the bed with a very loud "MEOW." He landed on the floor with a thud.

"OH!" Belinda said as she awakened. "Oh, Custard, thank you for waking me up. I had a very crowded dream about the Christmas Pageant! There were sheep and cows and a donkey and an ELEPHANT in the bed," she giggled. "No wonder there was no room for you!"

Belinda straightened her pillow and comforter. She curled up for one warm moment before starting her busy day.

"Howard," she said, "I don't know if You gave me that dream so I could practice, but I sure hope I don't have to be a sheep again. Last year I had to wear an itchy sheep costume and walk around on all fours like Custard." Sighing, she rolled over and said, "If You need me to be a sheep, I guess I can do that. But I would sure like to be an angel this year if that would be okay."

Giggling, she continued, "See You in church, Howard!" And off she went to her breakfast.

Sneaking a piece of bacon from the plate by the stove, Belinda munched happily, thinking about the day ahead of her. There would be church in the morning, but she didn't have to help with the Advent Wreath this week, thank goodness. Then lunch. Then maybe she could catch up on her Advent Calendar. And LAST, there would be the Christmas Pageant at church in the evening.

"Dad," said Belinda, "I have some questions about the pageant tonight."

"Okay," her father said. "Go for it!"

"First," said Belinda, "what if I don't want to be a sheep again this year? And second, what if I want to be an angel? And third, why do they call it The Christmas Miracle?"

"Wow," her father said. "Let's see: I can't tell you which part you will play tonight. But if you stop sneaking bacon and come to the table for breakfast, I can tell you why they call it The Christmas Miracle."

Making her way to the table at top speed, Belinda quickly bowed her head and waited patiently while Gramps said Grace. As soon as she heard "AMEN," she peeked at her father, still waiting for an answer.

Laughing just a little, Belinda's father explained: They called the pageant a miracle because there was so little preparation, but it always seemed to work anyway.

Her grandfather continued the explanation. "For as long as I can remember—even when I was a little boy—the Christmas Pageant just kind of happened," Gramps said. "One of the grown-ups at church invites all of the children to participate. The kids go to the Sunday School classroom and put on costumes: some shepherds, some wise men, some angels—even some sheep and a donkey."

Swallowing a bite of breakfast, Belinda's father picked up the story from there. "Some churches have lots of rehearsals," he said. "But we try to make sure that all the children know the story of the first Christmas. And the miracle is that it always works!"

Belinda thought she could help make a GREAT miracle as an angel. But if not an angel, she at least hoped to be promoted from sheep to shepherd!

After church, she worked hard on her Advent Calendar, bringing it up to date. "Well," she said to her father, "I don't think any of these are what Christmas is, but I think I'm getting closer!"

The day flew by, and before Belinda knew it, they were back at church. She was so excited about maybe being an angel that she unfastened her seat belt and started moving as soon as the car was parked.

Belinda's father and grandfather sank into a pew with delight, enjoying the candles and the quiet. They knew full well that "backstage" was anything but quiet. And they were so right!

Backstage was a frenzy of costumes and instructions. Two of Belinda's best friends were going to be shepherds, and Elizabeth's little sister, Lisa, was going to be a tiny angel. Belinda—lucky Belinda—was the talking angel. She was already walking around mumbling, "For behold I bring you tidings of great joy..."

At last it was time to begin. When an usher opened the door into the church for them, the children winked at each other in excitement. How proud their parents would be!

The shepherds took their places, then the wise men. Finally it was time for the angels to come forward. Until…

"Uh-oh," Belinda whispered to one of the wise men. "It looks like Lisa is frozen solid in the doorway."

Stage fright wasn't something that Belinda was familiar with, but she knew that the littlest angel was scared silly. The pageant had barely started, and the children behind Lisa couldn't even get past her to go through the doorway. It would be pretty silly if the wise men had to sneak around the angel and get there first!

Near the back of the church, Lisa's mother saw what had happened and started to get up. But Belinda's father put a hand out, saying, "Wait." He'd already seen Belinda reaching out to Lisa, and he recognized the struggle on his daughter's face. Belinda always wanted to do her best and loved to make her family proud. But her good heart was bigger than her pride. No way could she abandon that tiny angel. With a small bow to the audience and another to her family, she took Lisa's hand. Together, they walked down the long, empty aisle. The first and last of the angels.

Belinda hunkered down carefully to avoid damaging her wings. Then she wiped away the little girl's tears. Grownups looked on as the littlest angel and the most important angel stepped forward to bring the Christmas story to life, just as it was every year.

"The only thing that would've been better," said Belinda when they went out for ice cream after the pageant, "would've been if I could've carried Custard. An angel and a kitty would have been absolutely perfect!" But she winked at her father when she said it. She knew Custard would not have been able to resist getting into the act. And who knows what could have happened to The Christmas Miracle then?

After ice cream and hugs from her dad and Gramps, Belinda settled into her warm bed for the night. She was already thinking about drawing TWO angels on her Advent Calendar—a little one and a big one. "That will be perfect," she whispered to Custard. She wrapped her arm around him as they cuddled close on a cold winter night.

December 23: Sleigh Ride

So the littlest angel had stage fright! Has that ever happened to YOU? Just when you are going to tell a story or sing a song or do a special dance—BOING! Butterflies fly around in your tummy and you feel kind of sick. Yuck. It happens to lots of people—grown-ups too. But sometimes having a friend helps a lot. Do you think you would help someone who had butterfly troubles? I am hoping Belinda might get a special treat for being so brave. Let's see what happens next!

When dawn peeked over the windowsill of Belinda's room, she smiled and said, "Good morning, Howard! I had a very strange dream! I dreamed about the Christmas pageant and Baby Jesus and Santa and the North Pole. That's a little bit weird, but I guess it was all about Christmas!"

Petting Custard quietly, she walked to the window and looked out at December sunshine on newly fallen snow. "Howard," she said, "I remember the first December snow! It was right after the day when Custard stole a cookie," she giggled. "And Gramps promised a surprise! Howard, thank You for all the magic of December—the Baby Jesus magic and the Santa magic and the Christmas tree magic and ALL of it. And whatever the surprise is, thank you AHEAD OF TIME too! I love You and have a great day."

With that, she was off and running to the kitchen, with Custard still in her arms.

"Gramps," she said as she ran into his arms for a morning kiss. "Gramps, I remembered about the surprise and there aren't any days left and it MUST be today!"

"Good morning, Belinda," her grandfather chuckled. "I wondered when you'd remember. Your father asks me every morning and night if it's today!"

"AND IS IT?" Belinda asked. "Yes, it is indeed today," her grandfather said with a hug and his best laugh. "Just let me finish getting breakfast on the table and I'll tell you all about it."

And while they ate hot oatmeal with chopped up bits of apple, Belinda's grandfather told the story of the Christmas surprise.

"You see, Belinda," said her grandfather, "when I was a little boy, my parents still had horses. And at Christmas every year, my grandfather and my father and my Uncle Tom would hitch their horses to a single sleigh. The families would have the most incredible sleigh ride. We even stopped to see friends and neighbors along the way, dropping off homemade cookies."

Belinda's grandfather paused a moment to eat some oatmeal while it was still hot.

"Anyway," he continued. "After a while, there wasn't much open land around anymore, so my father sold the horses and the sleigh. But I never forgot what a sleigh ride was like."

He paused again, and Belinda thought she would scream with waiting. She was sure she knew what the surprise was now and was ready to burst with excitement.

"Until you and your father came to live here this year, I kind of gave up on the idea of sleigh rides. But it made me sad to think that you never knew what a sleigh ride was like, so I started calling people with horses. And I talked to people in other towns and asked around until I found someone who would take us on a sleigh ride."

For once, even Belinda was without words. Then, suddenly, the table came to life as she and her father talked at once. "When would they go? What should they wear? Would they be allowed to pet the horses?"

"Whoa!" said Belinda's grandfather. "This is worse than Belinda all by herself! Even she only asks three questions at a time."

Reaching into his wallet, Gramps pulled out an old, old picture. It was a little crumply and the colors had faded, but it showed Belinda's grandfather when he was very young. He stood beside a sleigh, with the horses' breath freezing in the cold. The boy smiled with huge saucer eyes as he looked at the horses and the sleigh. Belinda could see how excited he was. She put her little hand into her grandfather's big one and said, "Let's get ready, Gramps. I think we need a sleigh ride."

The ride to the farm where the horses lived felt like forever! They drove past gas stations and the town firehouse, and Belinda was pretty sure there were no horses in the firehouse! When they finally arrived, she tumbled out of the car, practically bouncing on springs from excitement!

The farmer was dressed in a warm coat, boots, and a wool hat. Belinda kind of hoped for a cowboy hat, but one look at the horses and she was silent for at least a whole minute!

Up and up and up she looked, and still there was more horse to see! "Look!" she whispered. "Horses never looked that huge to me on television."

As the farmer hitched the horses to the sleigh, the family climbed aboard. The driver had a snowy beard, and his skin was wrinkled from years spent outdoors. He didn't say much, but his blue eyes twinkled as he handed out warm blankets. With a wink at Belinda, he was ready to go at last. "All aboard!" he shouted, then he gave the reins a twitch and they were off.

"Ohhhhhhhh," said Belinda. "It's like ice skating and sledding and running at the same time!!"

Occasionally Belinda saw a rabbit or field mouse, looking for dinner or a warm place to sleep. "Hi, guys," Belinda whispered to the animals as the sleigh went flying along. "I won't forget to put food out for you on Christmas Eve! You can count on me!"

Looking up, Belinda saw that everything looked different from a sleigh. You could look up and see the sky, and you could reach out to touch tree branches as you whiz by. Belinda sighed a contented sigh.

As the family got used to the ride, Belinda began to sing "Jingle Bells." Soon, Sam, Gramps, and even the driver joined in, startling the bunnies and field mice back into the woods.

Right in the middle of a rousing version of "Deck the Halls," Belinda began sticking out her tongue and looking all around. "Look, it's starting to snow!" And indeed it was. Sam and Gramps smiled, knowing that the sleigh ride's magic was complete. Not only riding and singing, but a Christmas snow besides. Soon they returned to the farm.

Everyone thanked the driver, and Belinda thanked each of the horses as well. She walked around and gave them a careful pat, staying just where the driver told her. The horses were blowing lots of smoke. They had to go inside pretty quickly or they'd get chilled from standing still. Belinda's grandfather said, "Belinda, those horses are not the only ones that will get chilled if they don't go inside! Let's head for home and get some hot chocolate and homemade cookies!"

In the car on the way home, Belinda said, "I want to remember this Christmas for ever and ever, 'cause it has been the best Christmas in my whole life. So I think what I want for Christmas is something that helps me remember everything—the tree and The Nutcracker and the sleigh ride, and even Custard the Hero."

Sam said, "Well, you will have your Advent Calendar. So I guess we'd better go home and make sure you add the sleigh ride while it's fresh in your mind." And so she did.

December 24: Family

Did you ever have trouble sleeping because you were SO excited? Belinda thought she would be up all night after that sleigh ride, but instead she dreamed about horses and snowflakes and "Jingle Bells" and flying around like Santa himself! Do YOU ever dream about flying through the night like Santa? It's hard to imagine that there's anything left to make Christmas special for Belinda—but let's find out, just in case!

From the kitchen, Belinda could hear her favorite Christmas carol, "Oh Little Town of Bethlehem." Sitting straight up in bed, she looked at the calendar on the wall. She had marked each day off with a big red "X" all month long, and there were twenty-three red Xes. That meant today was CHRISTMAS EVE.

Part of her wanted to bounce out of bed and begin this most important day. Instead, she turned on her side, wrapped one arm around Custard, and whispered, "Good morning, Howard. Happy Almost Birthday to Baby Jesus! I know that it isn't MY birthday and I've already had so many special things. But if I could get just ONE thing for Christmas, it would be a hug from my mommy. I know she's far away, and it would be a lot. But I was thinking about how much You love Baby Jesus, and I know that my mommy loves me too. So if You could bring her home for Christmas, that would be the awesomest present ever."

Taking a deep breath, she said, "AND I love You bazillions! AMEN!"

With a last pat for Custard, Belinda was off and running.

Her father was in the kitchen, looking at a big list on the table. SO many things to do today! Peeking over his shoulder, Belinda saw "Tree, wrapping, crèche, food for the animals, cookies for Santa..." On and on!

"Whew," Belinda said. "We have so many things to do today! And I'm not quite finished with my Advent Calendar yet, so I better do that first?"

"Well," her father said, "why don't you go check on the present you made? Let me know if you need any paper or ribbon to wrap it. I'll finish breakfast while you do that, and we'll plan the rest of the day together!"

"I'll be back in one quick minute," Belinda called over her shoulder. In her room, she was careful to close the door to keep Custard out. He'd already had one adventure with her glue pot and sparklies, and she wanted to wrap her presents before he "helped" her any more.

Belinda rolled the present for her parents carefully. She used the scissors and tape and paper and ribbon she'd hidden under her bed a week ago. She wrapped the present in no time. Then she wrapped her special present for Grandmother—a drawing of her very own self in the green dress she had worn to The Nutcracker! Finally Belinda placed the presents safely on a shelf in her closet, closed the closet door and raced back downstairs to see what would happen next.

While her father finished making breakfast, Belinda checked out the box of Christmas ornaments in the living room. She was a little sad to see the angel. She remembered that last year her mommy had lifted her up so that she could put the angel on top of the tree. Missing her, she looked at other ornaments that she loved. She saw a red star she'd made out of clay at school, and a crooked green tree cut from construction paper. There were even things her parents had made when they were children. All of the ornaments had stories to tell. She loved being able to help hang them on Clarence, their very special Christmas tree.

After breakfast, Belinda and her father carefully unwrapped the pieces of the Nativity scene. Belinda carefully placed the wise men and angels in the crèche. She remembered the fun of being an angel in the Christmas pageant.

She knew that they would not put the Baby Jesus in the manger until Christmas morning. Her father put the tiny baby in a safe place on the mantel until the time came.

Fixing food to place outside for the animals was the next job on the list. Belinda helped make small bowls of food for the birds and squirrels and raccoons that would celebrate Christmas in their own way. She smiled as she thought about the Baby Jesus and the animals in the stable. She wished she could feed some sheep and a donkey, but she settled for the beautiful birds that lived near her house in the wintertime.

While Belinda and her father were busy with the crèche and fixing animal feasts, Gramps was putting lights on the tree. That was the hardest part of decorating the tree, and he was very particular! He told Belinda that he liked to put lots and lots and lots of lights on their tree—one hundred lights for every foot! Belinda tried to do the arithmetic in her head very fast: 100 hundred lights for every foot times ten feet… but Gramps was faster. He said their tree needed one thousand lights!!

When Gramps stopped to get more lights, Belinda carefully poked her nose into the tree. "I love the smell of Christmas trees!" she whispered. "And especially, you, Clarence! You're not as big as the Rockefeller Center tree, but you're perfect for our house." Sniffing again, she said, "I think the Rockefeller Center tree would probably go right through our roof, so you are just the right tree for us!"

Just when Belinda was starting to think about lunch, she heard a car coming up the driveway. She wondered who was visiting. Her father and Gramps looked at each other and smiled big smiles.

"Who is it?" Belinda asked.

"Why don't you go and see," her father said.

Running to the door, Belinda peeked out and saw a big black car. An older gentleman was opening the back door, and someone was getting out.

"Look, it's Grandmother!" Belinda shouted as she saw her grandmother emerge from the car.

Before she made it to the car to greet her grandmother, Belinda saw another door open. She wondered who else could be coming to her house.

At first, she couldn't see who it was. She could only see bright red boots with high heels. Whoever it was had put their feet out but they were hiding behind the door!

Belinda turned around and looked at her father and looked at Gramps. She was confused. Who had come to visit them but hid behind the door of the car?

And then she saw a face with green eyes just like hers and curly red hair just like hers peeking around the door.

"Mommy, Mommy, Mommy, Mommy!" she shrieked.

She started to cry, frozen to the spot. After all this time, she thought she would run so fast to her mother, but she was as frozen as the little angel in the Christmas pageant.

The next thing Belinda knew, she didn't have to move at all. Her mommy had picked her up and held her like she would never let go again.

As Belinda hugged her mother tighter and tighter, her father wrapped both his wife and Belinda inside a whole-family-hug. They had waited so long for this moment.

As soon as she had her breath, Belinda had her usual three questions. "Mommy, did Daddy know you were coming today? And did Grandmother drive you all the way from Germany? And are you home to stay?"

“Yes, Belinda,” her mother said. “Your father knew I would arrive today, but we wanted you to be surprised.”

Smiling at her mother, Belinda’s mother continued. “Grandmother and her driver picked me up at the airport in New York and drove me here. It’s a very long flight from Germany, and I was grateful to have time with your grandmother and an easy trip from the airport.”

“As for your last question, yes, I am home to stay. I missed you and your father and Grandmother and Gramps and even Custard! And we are all going to have the best Christmas ever.”

“Oh,” Belinda said. “It is already the best Christmas ever! But I don’t know if I ever found the answer to your question.”

“Let’s go inside and get warm,” her father said. “You can show your mommy all the hard work you’ve done on your Advent Calendar. And you can tell her your ideas about What It Is That Makes It Christmas.”

Without putting Belinda down, her mother reached into the trunk and pulled out a special present. It was a gift that Grandmother had brought from New York. Carrying both the little girl and the present, she walked into the house.

Soon everyone settled in the living room near the tree, drinking coffee or tea or hot chocolate. Grandmother had even brought some special cookies and snacks from New York, so they munched while they talked.

Belinda sat as close to her mother as she could get without climbing inside her skin. She beamed at her with a smile so big, it almost made her face hurt.

"Belinda," her father said, "would you like to go get your Advent Calendar? You could tell your mom and Grandmother and Gramps your ideas about What It Is that Makes It Christmas."

Belinda was gone and back in seconds. She settled herself near her mother again, with the calendar in her hands.

Her mom looked at all the pictures Belinda had drawn. She could easily see how much thought she'd given to the question.

"Belinda, you took my question very seriously," she said. "But it's important that you know that none of us knows the whole answer. We know the story of Baby Jesus. But what we are all trying to figure out is: What does Christmas mean to us every day? Not just in December, but all year long."

"YES!" Belinda shouted. "I could have just drawn twenty-four pictures of Baby Jesus. But when I first started, I thought Christmas was about the tree and the snow and the stockings and all of the stuff we do at Christmastime. But then I thought about lots of other things, like you can see in my pictures."

Pointing at the tenth day on the calendar, she said, "I thought about loving Custard so much I thought I'd explode when he got lost. And I thought about how the firefighters love to deliver toys to children. And I thought about how I missed you, and how much Gramps loves us.

"But mostly it's about Baby Jesus who came to Earth on Christmas to teach us about love. And Baby Jesus is about Howard. He loved us so much that He loaned us Baby Jesus, even though He would miss him a lot, like I missed you."

"So what you're saying, Belinda," her mother said with a little choke in her voice, "is that you answered the question. You found Christmas—in a big way. That Christmas is about love from Howard, from Baby Jesus, from Gramps and your Grandmother, and your dad and the firefighters—and from you too!"

"I think that's more than three," said Belinda. "But that's okay. Maybe next Christmas I'll ask questions in SIXES instead of threes!"

Laughing, they worked together to decorate the tree and hang their stockings. They put out cookies for Santa and opened one present apiece. All the while, Belinda barely moved a single inch from her mother's side.

And when bedtime came, she whispered the biggest prayer of all to Howard: "Thank You, Howard! Thank You for my mommy. And thank You for loaning Baby Jesus to us even though You knew that You would miss Him, just like I missed my mommy. See You in the morning!"

And while she was sleeping, deep in the darkness and silence of a cold December night, Christmas came at last.

December 25: Christmas

I don't know about you, but I am going to miss reading about Belinda every day. I wonder if you drew an Advent Calendar too, and if you had a lot of the same ideas as Belinda. Lucky for us, there is ONE MORE DAY of this story—and it is, of course, the best day of all. Shhh—it's Christmas!

When Belinda awoke on Christmas morning, she heard only the quiet purring of her cat. No Christmas carols from the kitchen. No sleigh bells on the rooftop. And yet she knew. Her heart was bursting with the good news of Christmas—so many good things to celebrate. She was off and running before Custard could even wake up.

Standing politely outside her parents' bedroom door, she knocked quietly. She knew it was pretty early and still very dark, but it was, after all, Christmas morning!

Her parents told her to come in, and she jumped into the warm bed with them for hugs and Christmas wishes. But she couldn't stay still very long, and soon they were grabbing their warm robes and slippers.

As he always did, her father went to the living room first to turn on the tree lights. Her mother gently knocked on doors to awaken Gramps and Grandmother.

Tiptoeing quietly down the stairs, Belinda gasped when she saw how beautiful the tree was. The thousand lights sparkled in the dark morning. It reminded her of the Christmas Pageant and the star that sparkled in the dark sky so long ago.

In minutes, her parents had coffee and tea and hot chocolate ready for everyone in the living room. Belinda's big moment was at hand.

Carefully, tenderly, Belinda placed the tiny Baby Jesus in the manger. She said softly, "Welcome, Baby Jesus. Thank You for coming and Happy Birthday!"

Looking around she said, "Does that mean it's time for PRESENTS now?"

The grown-ups laughed and said that it was, indeed, time for presents. And the first present was for Belinda from Grandmother. The box was the most beautiful robin's egg blue, with a white ribbon all around it.

Belinda said sternly, "You already gave me a present, Grandmother! My beautiful dress and The Nutcracker!"

"Well," her grandmother chuckled, "I know that you like things that come in threes. Your third present is actually a present in progress. We'll have to finish it after Christmas, but I think you'll figure it out!"

With that, Belinda couldn't wait any longer. She ripped off the ribbon, opened the box, and saw the most beautiful charm bracelet in the world. There was a Christmas tree charm, and a stocking charm. There were cookies and a church. And even a little cat that looked like Custard.

"It's my Advent Calendar," Belinda breathed. "Oh Grandmother, it is beautiful! Would you put it on me right away?"

"Of course," Grandmother said. "We'll have to get some more charms because I couldn't keep up with all the pictures you were making. But after Christmas, we'll order more charms so you have a reminder of every single day."

"Belinda," said her mother, "I have a surprise for you too. Grandmother and I talked about how much you loved seeing The Nutcracker…

With that, she handed a bright, silvery box to Belinda, who jingled her bracelet as she opened it.

"Pink shoes?" Belinda asked. "Soft pink shoes??"

Her mother chuckled. "They are ballet slippers that you can wear when you start taking ballet lessons. Would you like to try them on?"

Tissue paper and silvery box and bunny slippers went flying as Belinda reached for the soft pink ballet slippers.

Belinda's mother smiled as she helped Belinda to put the soft pink slippers on one at a time. They smiled happy smiles at each other, enjoying the feel of the soft slippers on the little girl feet.

"WOW!" said Belinda! Jingling her bracelet and taking tiny dancer steps she ran to her room to find the present she had made for her mom and dad.

Bowing to her parents with pride, Belinda gave them the picture she had made. She told the story of Custard's leap into the glue pot and how he managed to cover himself with sparklies. Lots of laughter filled the room. Custard himself, though, wasn't looking all that happy as he saw the picture admired by one and all without a single word of thanks to him!

Grandmother beamed with surprise at her present: a drawing. "Oh my goodness!" she said. "I can't imagine anything better than a drawing of Belinda in her Nutcracker dress drawn by Belinda herself. Thank you very much!"

Gramps gave the next present. He reached under the tree for a carefully wrapped box and gave it to Belinda with a smile.

When Belinda unwrapped it, she found a picture of her dad and herself on the sleigh ride. They were smiling and singing "Jingle Bells" and having a wonderful time.

Belinda hugged her grandfather with an extra squeeze. "I love it, Gramps. I will never forget the sleigh ride. Now I can hang this picture up in my room, and Mom can see the sleigh ride too. Thank you!!"

With so much excitement and so many hugs going around, Belinda's father thought maybe he should save his present for later. But he'd been working on it for a long time, and it was a little bit unusual.

He looked at his wife and reached for the guitar that leaned against the fireplace. "Belinda," he said, "do you think that you could stand just one more present before we make our Christmas breakfast?"

"Is it a song? Is it a Christmas carol? Is it 'Jingle Bells'?" she asked, bouncing around the room. "I LOVE to sing Christmas carols!!"

Belinda's dad smiled at his wife as he began gently strumming the guitar. "Well, Belinda, it's actually a song your mom and I wrote just for you because we loved the way you went about Finding Christmas. And nobody knows this song yet but us—so would you like to hear it?"

"WOULD I WOULD I WOULD I?" She sang, sitting down between her parents. "A song for me called 'Finding Christmas'? I don't know how much more Christmas I can hold!"

And with a gentle smile, her father began playing and singing the song that they would soon be able to sing as a family.

Belinda invites you to visit
www.RedMittenBooks.com
to hear the song just as Belinda's father
played and sang it.

Finding Christmas

It's not the tree that makes it Christmas.
It's not the stockings in a row.
It's not the reindeer on the rooftop
or even sparkling Christmas snow.

Do you want to know? I can tell you
where the magic of Christmas starts.
Not the presents you see
underneath the tree,
but the Presence you feel
in your hearts.

I used to think that it was Santa
with his red suit and ho-ho-ho.
But now I know he's a reminder
of Christmas love from long ago.

I know the part about the stable.
About the wise men and the star,
the lowly shepherds on the hillside
who heard the angels from afar.

Do you want to know? I can tell you
all the rest of the story too.
With no room at the inn,
did He look within?
Is His Presence the light
that's in you?

I've heard the songs that tell the story,
that unto us a Child was born.
The Lamb of God, laid in a manger among the
sheep on Christmas morn.

Do you want to know? I can tell you
how to play your own Christmas part.
Share the love that He brings
as your glad heart sings
of the Presence you feel
in your heart.

Words and music by Barbara Escher
Arranged and performed by Roger Sullins

About the Author

Barbara Escher fell in love with Christmas at an early age. She grew up in Philadelphia and loved seeing the city come alive with light and color as Christmas approached.

People think of Philadelphia as the land of soft pretzels and Independence Hall. But it was also the home of a historic department store where a giant Christmas tree changed colors in time to organ music while children craned their necks in wonder.

Many years later, Barbara looks back on her passion for Christmas and remembers the years she spent teaching and creating stories. First for every kid on her block. And later for a classroom and her own children. Even when she helped companies craft their success stories, she often found a way to sneak a little Christmas in the back door! After all, telling stories and making things come to life whether it was a business or stuffed toy had a lot in common.

One day Barbara decided that she wanted to tell a very special kind of story. So she stopped running a business and began writing the children's book that had been in her head for so long.

Today, Barbara lives in Tampa, Florida with her husband Joe and Hope, their Havanese lapdog. She still loves Christmas and delights in decorating her Christmas tree with ornaments her children made long ago.

Tampa is less than an hour from the Gulf Beaches, and Barbara loves to dip her toes in the waves when she isn't writing. She also loves spending time with her children, grandchildren, and grand-pets (three dogs, three cats, and a turtle named Michelangelo).

When she was a little girl, Barbara read every book she could get her hands on from the Betsy-Tacy stories to all-time-favorite Nancy Drew. Today, if you came to visit, you would see that she still has a book open in every room of the house!

Barbara's next book will follow her heroine, Belinda, on a new adventure.
Watch RedMittenBooks.com for more information.